THE HISTORY

OF THE WORLD

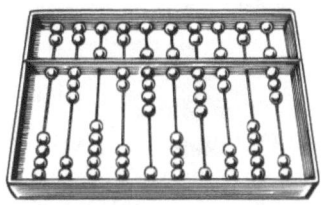

NP Novellas

Set 2:

Rowany de Vere and a Fair Degree of Frost
— **Chaz Brenchley**
The Hamlet — **Joanna Corrance**
The Creator — **Aliya Whiteley**
Cities Are Forests Waiting to Happen — **Cécile Cristofari**
The History of the World — **Simon Morden**

Set 1:

Universal Language — **Tim Major**
Worldshifter — **Paul Di Filippo**
May Day — **Emma Coleman**
Requiem for an Astronaut — **Daniel Bennett**
Rose Knot — **Kari Sperring**
On Arcturus VII — **Eric Brown**
Fish! — **Ida Keogh**
My Mother Murdered the Moon — **Stephen Deas**
Visions of Ruin — **Mark West**
Entropy of Loss — **Stewart Hotston**
Telling the Bees — **Emma K. Leadley**
The Blackhart Blades — **David Gullen**

THE HISTORY OF THE WORLD

OF THE WORLD

Simon Morden

NewCon Press
England

First published in the UK August 2025 by
NewCon Press
41 Wheatsheaf Road,
Alconbury Weston,
Cambs, PE28 4LF

NPN32 (limited edition hardback)
NPN33 (paperback)

10 9 8 7 6 5 4 3 2 1

ISBN:
978-1-917735-09-4 (hardback)
978-1-917735-10-0 (paperback)

Cover layout and design by Ian Whates
incorporating an image by AstroGraphics Visuals

Editorial meddling and typesetting by Ian Whates

ONE
0.9999999999c

This was PurLeeDah's home system. This was the one Corbyn had passed through so long ago, dreaming about whatever sentient ramships dreamt about, all the while being bombarded by increasingly frantic messages of greeting and offers of exchange of knowledge from the inhabited, civilised, industrialised planet in orbit around the system's primary.

It was the same system that then fell into acrimony and war, and afterwards bent its entire resources to designing, building, and launching its first and only light speed spaceship to chase after him and ask him why he'd ignored them.

Their ship – the Great Honour – had one advantage he didn't possess. A D-jump mechanism, folding space between two points to make the distance negligible. His ship – UNDSP-14 CORBYN, indistinguishable from him, his body, his home, his person – had one advantage the Great Honour didn't possess. Resilience. By the time he became aware of the vessel alongside, it was a failing wreck. PurLeeDah, he rescued. The D-jump device, he salvaged.

The other crew? There had been other crew, and he and her had rationalised abandoning them to become stardust because of their complicity in a centuries-long plot to murder her in case she came back with the wrong answer.

Now he had returned her to her world, so that she could see what had become of those who'd selected her as ambassador and inquisitor, and most likely, martyr. Subjectively, for him and her, years had passed. Subjectively, for the culture that had sent the Great Honour into the deep black, the passage of time was a little harder to estimate.

When he'd been roused from his slumber, he was running a gamma of three hundred. An unconscionable velocity. He had come to terms with the likelihood that Earth, old Earth, his starting place and origin, had altered irrevocably: any residual bonds of fealty that might tie them together had crumbled away. He had knowledge of all of human history up to his departure point. Or at least, all of human history which was deemed useful to tell him, good and bad: he knew it was unlikely that there was anyone left who might either know of him, or the people who commissioned his making, Corbyn being merely the fourteenth of his line.

PurLeeDah's world was at least a thousand years in the past. Probably more. Would there be anyone to remember her? He had broached the subject with her. She was, by training, a historian. She was realistic about the survival of memory. As she was about their own survival.

Corbyn was excellent at calculations, down to the lowest register of decimal places, and yet, if he made even a marginal error here, he and his precious cargo were going to die before they knew they were going to die. He had been built with the capacity to feel fear – his human creators deemed it an utterly essential corrective to hubris – and at the precise moment after transition, he was terrified. He came in over the plane of the ecliptic, but that didn't mean his projected path was debris free, and he was coming in hot. His velocity, in the system's space-time frame, was a metre a second below light speed. Every collision would be energetic, and that was the point of his trajectory from outer system to inner system. Always sunwards.

It was the only way to slow down. He needed the imparted momentum. To turn, to fire up his fusion engines and decelerate as God and Heinlein intended, needed him to be below point eight c, at the very least. Otherwise, the solar wind would chew him up and spit him out, much as it had done the Great Honour.

But also, if he hit anything more substantial than a grain of sand? He was moving at a speed that made him a relativistic kill vehicle, a weapon dreamed about and never used in his timeline. This was the risk. And it would be the risk every single transit. To end his existence in a flash that might be seen halfway across the galaxy.

To complicate matters further, he was more-or-less blind. The sky ahead of him was painted in x-rays. Behind him, space was so far in the infrared that it was barely above background. Subjective reality was compressed to a point of incomprehension. Any and all information was shifted so far outside its original frequency as to require vast computational power to deconvolve it, and in the process, degrade and alter it. The only way he knew the universe still existed were the stars winking in and out of existence as he encountered them in the orthogonal plane.

His first transit through PurLeeDah's system would take a little over twenty seconds. At the end of that twenty seconds, he would jump back to the start and do it again. He would have to make the same transit thousands of times.

He could find no radio signals, from any sources. Perhaps they had progressed beyond that. He would have to wait and see.

Everything was being done for her – done to her – and for now she had no option but to comply. Head up, look right, look left, arms out, back down, breathe in, no: *really* breathe in. Dressed and painted and laced and anointed. Pulled this way and that.

And she was grateful. It left her free to think, a quiet core of furious calm. Despite them making her seem special, the centre of attention, she realised that she was simply passing through the same rites and rituals as every woman before her had. Every woman after her would eventually do the same. It was simply her turn. It was the way of things. She was not special. That was the deeper meaning.

And when she ran, she was not expected to run fast. When she hid, she was not expected to vanish. When she fought, she was not expected to be victorious. That was also the way of things.

It had been, it was, it will be.

The hands finally retreated. She was resplendent. A wild animal. Hair braided and knotted tight to her scalp before falling between her shoulder blades as a rope tied with thongs and fetishes. Black ash and red ochre carefully applied in time-worn patterns across her face and neck. Leather and feathers and fur wrapped around her. A chimera. Of nature, but unnatural.

She wasn't tall, but she stood tall. She liked this. She was supposed to like this, for certain, but she still felt stronger than she ought, more cunning than even her usual quick wits permitted. She noticed things, sensing – seeing, tasting, smelling, hearing – things that were normally obscured. She'd been told that this would happen, that the drops and tinctures that had stung her eyes and embittered her tongue would change her, would make her more beast than not. It was still a surprise to find it was true, and not part of the allegory.

The rest of it was allegory, for certain. She – prey. He – hunter. She would seek to evade him, and he would seek to track her, and bring her down, and bring her back. How much evasion was necessary to complete her part of the story was moot: there were social mores to consider, and also mutual understandings. It was supposed to have a degree of difficulty, and there were tales told between women that she had overheard, and had probably been meant to overhear, about those who had made it too easy to be caught, and conversely, those who had made it oh so hard and had started their relationships with rancour and resentment. He had to prove himself sufficiently worthy. She had to prove herself sufficiently tameable. The sufficiency, the enoughness, was the goal. Extremes were, if not taboo, certainly frowned on.

It was the way of things.

She was led – surrounded by a ring of bodies that moved as one, her own personal cage at which she always remained in the centre – from where she had been dressed to where the hunt would start. It was still dark, their way lit with clay lamps and waxed wicks guarded by bone panes. The women started calling. Barking, crowing, howling, chirruping. In return, the distant men began their drums and their bells and their flutes.

She hadn't known how she would feel. She had imagined fear, a rising panic that would make her limbs tremble and her heartbeat race and skip. What she experienced, in the centre of that circle, was different. She felt mighty. If she was going to take her part in this story, she would tell it her own way. She would run fast but straight. Let him catch her if he could.

To the north, through the trees they used for coppicing, was rising ground. Sloping hills and the wild wood. Deeply incised valleys with rocky, rushing streams. On the tops, tough shrubs and bare pavements. An uninterrupted view of the bowl of the sky. Let it be there, her fur and feathers blown breathless by the wind, skinned knees and scuffed palms, brought down in an exhausted tangle to lie there until they both grew cold and serious.

That would be enough. Surely, that would be enough.

The noise grew into a cacophony, each side – her side, his side, there always needed to be a balance – growing louder, not to drown the other out but to match it for volume. This was a celebration, not a competition. Everyone knew their parts in the pageant.

And still it rose: feet stamping, hand clapping, calling, ululations, the shrieking of overblown pipes and double-thunder of the drums. Too much was too much. Excess would lead to ambition, and ambition to ruin, eventually. The sound receded, as a storm backs and treetops cease their roaring and swinging. Not choreographed, but understood. They had approached a line, and they had pulled away from it.

It was in the quiet murmuring that her circle opened. His stayed closed, and would do for a little while, until she was out of sight.

The path ahead weaved its way through the houses and hurdles on its way to the hills. Above her, the pin-bright stars turned. She rose on the balls of her feet, testing her legs, weighing their ability to keep her moving. Yes, there were the familiar twinges, the tightness of the old burn on her right foot, the cuts she'd received on her thigh a month ago from nothing more than an enraged fowl with murder in its tiny breast.

Whatever she had been dosed with, though, made everything needle-sharp and discrete. The dark shadow where the path dove into the woods rushed towards her, and everything else receded. The first reds of dawn limned the high clouds. Now. Now.

She ran. Slowly at first, no faster than a brisk walk, then an easy transition into a loping gait. She would not hare off, tire herself, and cause a shameful and brief chase. She knew where she wanted to reach before being caught. Did he? What if he didn't agree? He was quick. But he'd also not want the chase to over too soon. Where was the worth in that? They would dance around that point later.

The trees closed over her. The path was still well-trodden and wide, rutted from cart wheels and smoothed over again

11

by sleds, pale mud against the almost-black of the undergrowth. Tree roots made hard wooden steps, and she had to lift her knees high.

Had he been released already? She remembered that she was playing as prey. Now then, a little speed. Onwards, towards the hills. She couldn't hear him behind her, even with her preternatural hearing. But also, the only sounds she was making were her breath, and the soft crush of her feet against dirt of the path. His pursuit would be more or less silent, until it was over.

There was a structure in the woods. It had once been a tower, so it was thought, wide at the base and narrow at the top, hollow for most of its length, and fallen long ago. Its roots were vast, and its pinnacle a fragment a mile away. Every child, at some point, would ask what it had been for, and every child received the same answer: when we can make our own tower that stands a mile in the sky, we will know what this one was for.

Perhaps it had been built in among the trees. Perhaps the trees had come later. Perhaps the tower builders had cleared the forest, only to see it return. Perhaps the trees had dragged the tower down because such a feat of construction smacked of unwarranted excess and it caused an imbalance. Even while this last was not true, it was most likely the truest: the tower was lying on its side, broken, so its standing must have been an offence.

The path passed between two sections. They loomed, even though they were a hundred yards away to both left and right. Huge, thick walls rising above the canopy. A flat arch spanning the distance. The rock-that-was-not-rock was too smooth to climb, too hard to drive even iron tools into, too high to get a rope over.

Not for the first time, she wondered who these people were, how had they lived, where they went, and why no one else seemed to want to talk about them.

Her pace had slowed. That was not the plan. The sky was lightening and the obstacles in her way were clearer than ever. She surged forward and felt her feathers strain and stretch against her skin.

The ground began to slope up: gradually at first, just enough that she needed to raise her head to keep sight of the path as it dwindled into a track, the undergrowth encroaching with heavy autumn grasses that rattled off her ankles. Then steeper, the foot-worn passage narrow and stony after rains had washed down the soil. She found herself bounding from side to side with each stride, planting her feet on the verges. Graceful still, strong still, wild still.

And even though the trees grew shorter and more wind-blown, she had entered the deep wood, beyond what they used for pasture and lumber and fuel. It was where the hunters crept, strung bows in hand, sharp arrows at their waist. Where the wise women and cunning men searched and noted and gathered. Where the shepherds drove their flocks in spring to the high pastures beyond, and returned with the first snows, skin-backed and stinking.

She knew this way. Travelled it often enough to know its rises and turns. Never felt the danger of it, and always felt the release when she emerged on the tops to breathe the cold, ragged air. She had hefted herself not to the warm, still lowland but to the hardy high ground. Her choices, deliberate and unconscious, to run here rather than anywhere else, had already been made by her younger self.

If it was her own approval she sought, she gave it gladly.

The stunted trees thinned and shrank. Here was her big sky, growing larger by the moment, until it burst out on her and her heart swelled and her breath caught in her throat. She was one with the world and the world was one with her. The track dissolved into a dozen little tracklets, scurrying away. One and one only headed towards the first summit. She held to her word, that she would run straight with no deception, and struck out across the ever-rising ground.

She hadn't once looked behind her. Because, she realised, what he was doing wasn't important – he would catch up with her, inevitably, foreordained: the time before that moment was her own. Possibly the last time that was her own, ever, before the demands of life pulled down on her like a filling bucket.

Run, then. Run. Keep running.

She crested the hill, and the horizon rose. A shallow col separated one height from another greater one, with the land sloping down either side before ending in a tumble of rock and water and wood. Hard stone jutted out from under tough grasses, grey against the green. A flock of goats grazed among the hard stems and seed heads, and her sudden appearance made them bleat and scatter.

A herdsman unfolded himself from the ground, a thing more feral than her. He stood and watched, thick staff planted between his feet, knuckles wrapped around the weighted head. She curved her path around him, giving him due respect and caution. His hooded head turned to follow her, but that was all. She must know him, and he must know her, because their community was small enough to make that a certainty, but she didn't know who it was, and in her state, fur-clad and feather-trimmed, face painted and hair flying, would he know her?

But he would not interfere unless his flock was threatened, and she would not ask him for assistance, or anything. Why would she? She was a beast, and he, despite his appearance, was not. She: a fleeting thing; he: as old as the hills.

At the top of the next rise stood another structure, much younger than the fallen tower, much cruder, simply a shoulder-high ring-wall of flattish stones stacked one on the other, interlocking and pressing down on the previous course, with one narrow opening held apart by tall sarsens. Made and endlessly remade, a place of rough shelter and that was all.

Beyond, the land spread out like fabric, falling and rising and never ending. This was as far as she'd ever gone. She turned to face the way she'd come.

There he was. The distant goats flew and wheeled again. His pursuit of her was as steady as her flight from him. Now she had stopped, the distance between them closed. And now she had stopped, she could feel the first aches of fatigue, the first deepness of breath. If she stayed stopped, then this would still be enough, yes? To the edge of her known world.

A sliver of the sun rose behind her, an arc, golden and fierce. Surely a sign. Of what? Of something, for certain.

She threw her head back, to stare at the pale blue sky above, before spinning around and facing the way she had never gone, and never would.

There, out of nowhere, from zenith to horizon, shone the brightest blue light she had ever seen. A line. An arrow. A cut in the sky, tearing towards the sun, not quite reaching it. Along its length, almost bright enough to cast its own shadow. It left spots in her vision, dark stripes where she glimpsed it, and reflexively, she reached out her hand to shield herself.

The feathers on her arm ruffled.

If the rising sun was a sign, then this, surely, was also a sign. Again, of what, she didn't know. But there was a new light ahead of her, calling her on, pointing the way.

He was gaining rapidly. He had not yet caught her. She turned and turned again. The familiar sun. The blue line of light. She stumbled away from the herdsman's stone shelter, barely aware of what she was doing. Her feet found the downslope, away into the valley below, smooth at first and then steeper, a shoulder of scree that slipped and slid with her, then steeper still and she almost fell into a cliff-bounded ravine, all tangled trees and moss-grown boulders calved from the heights.

Her feet had too little grip. She could not go upslope. She hung on to a sapling that bent under her weight, and judged the distance to the next below her. She let go and slithered down, and then to the next, and the next.

The light, her guiding light, had gone behind the valley walls. She would have to climb up and out to the next peak to see it again. And she would. She would find a way, and that meant staying ahead of her pursuer.

Her costume was battered, much like her. She was bruised by the descent, scratched and grazed and whipped. Her form was revealed where the feathers and fur had ripped away, and the paint had streaked off. If she was to escape, it would be as her, not as something else.

And she had never thought of escaping until that moment.

The valley eased as it reached its bottom, but the river that had cut it had dug abruptly further: at that point, a channel twenty, thirty feet down in a slot that was only a few terrifying feet wide.

Could she jump it? As she gauged the distance, she could hear him above her, crashing and clattering down towards her. If she didn't try, this would end here, and now she didn't want it to end it would feel a little like death, wouldn't it?

She looked down into the gorge again. The depth was the only thing that made the crossing perilous. If she backed up, ran, and hit her mark, she would fly across and land safely on the other side.

It would be too much. She was already over the line into excess – this feat would turn her into one of those women, who were endlessly complained about, the difficult ones. And suddenly, she was with them, was them. Her life was mapped out for her on a small square of cloth – as was his, and surely he had to be having the same thoughts as her, his life ruled by different strictures but as confined as hers.

The blue light in the heavens told her that there was more beyond the frayed hem of her knowledge than she could dream of, and she did dream. A lot.

He was close. Soon all of this would become moot. She would be caught, and they would go back together. Past the silent, watching herdsman, judging her for not running faster, further, truer, away from a life that would kill her slowly with comfort and hardship and happiness and sorrow, but would kill her all the same because it did everyone.

There was a fallen tree across the gorge. It was old, covered in moss, probably rotten to the core. But it was only a few yards away and hadn't been purposefully hiding. She would risk it.

As she stood at one end of the trunk, one foot on its worryingly tight circumference, she wondered if some of these pursuits ended in failure. Did she get away? Did she, or he, die? Or both?

Did they both run off into the sunset, never to be seen again?

No one talked about those. It was impossible for her to know if it ever happened.

One, two, three, four steps. A slight wobble in the middle as the trunk sagged under her weight, a larger one at the end which saw her sprawl into the unearthed bowl of tree roots and hang on tight, toes scrabbling until she made solid ground.

More of her costume came away. She was becoming a girl again, no more, no less.

Her back was to the gorge, her head aimed upwards, searching the scarp for possible routes up, when he finally appeared behind her.

"Stop. Stop." He could barely get his words out. He was all but spent, but he was able to summon the holy incantation of: "Enough."

Her guts tightened on hearing it, and she bared her teeth. Of course it was enough. That didn't mean it would ever be enough for her. Her opinion, however, wasn't to be considered. She turned, not knowing where her fury needed to be directed.

"You saw it. You saw it."

He was doubled over, bleeding hands on his knees. "Saw what?"

"The light. You saw the light. In the east. It was…" she hesitated. What was it? "A sign." She sounded more certain than she felt. Here in the gap between the valley walls, which even the sun scorned, the blue line was more an idea than a manifest reality.

"I saw only the sun."

He had been facing the light the whole time that he'd chased her over the tops. He had seen it, and he was lying. Sudden, new things should not exist in their world, and yet, and yet.

Any respect, and feeling, and hope, for a life with this boy was gone in an instant. She was disgusted. Their fates a moment ago had been utterly entwined. Now they stood unravelled and unattached.

Still she felt compelled to give him one last chance, even though she was a believer and he was not.

"Come with me, and we'll find it together."

He finally straightened up, bowing his back and wincing at the pain. "We belong over here. People are waiting for us."

"What about those who never came back? What about them?"

"What? Are you mad?"

She was startled to find that she was. She was brimming with excess. With risk. With adventure. She'd crossed a line, metaphorical and geographical and cosmological. She was, by any fair assessment, mad.

"Yes," she said, and turned to her left, to track the gorge upstream and see if there was a manageable path back up onto the tops beyond. Eastward.

"You can't do this."

"I can. I can do this."

He didn't follow her. Whatever concoctions they had given her had worn off. She was just a young woman dressed in the tattered remains of an animal costume, an animal that had never even existed. She was tired and sore and thirsty. And filled with a spark of fire that, if it had a colour, would have been blue.

Two
0.999999999c

Corbyn had spent many days trying to find the right analogy to explain the situation to PurLeeDah. The best he could come up with was firing dried peas at the front of an express train in the hope of making it stop at the station, but he didn't know if her culture included peas, trains or stations. Still, he would try in the limited time they had together.

He didn't have to wake her – for her, even the dilated time spent in her scavenged module was reduced to nothingness by her inhabiting her sleep tank – but he wanted to. He needed to tell her that this would take some time, during which the sparse resources she relied on to keep her alive would dwindle further without hope of them being renewed. It remained to be seen whether they would last the course.

He had turned the gravity on in the module – such a novelty to be able to do that, and he didn't understand the physics of the circuitry hidden inside the black box, much like he didn't understand the physics behind the D-jump mechanism. If either one of them broke, he would have to attempt a repair, without much hope of success.

The lights on her sleep tank cycled from amber to green. Not that he was in her module with her, because he was a kilometre-long spaceship with a rest mass of seven hundred and fifty tonnes. But one of his spider-like maintenance bots was, tucked up in a corner and plugged into the power supply. It was his eyes, and if necessary, his hands.

The translucent gel pumped away and she emerged from the slime, coughing and gasping. This was normal. He'd even experienced it himself, though he was still at a loss as to how that had been possible, how the Great Honour had co-opted his sleeping mind to inhabit an ill-formed flesh mannequin, a genderless drone, and tried to get him to mend the ruined sections forward of the crew quarters. Again and again.

He'd had a body, no matter how crude, just for a while. He remembered those sensations: cold, pain, awkwardness. That was what it meant to be human.

She sat up in her tank, wiped the residual slime from her face, from around her lips.

"Corbyn?"

He used the module's speakers to reply.

"PurLeeDah. I have an update for you. This should not take long."

"Are we in orbit yet?"

"We are a very long way from orbit. We are currently on transit one hundred and eighty seven. Deceleration is marginal but measurable. My scheme is working as intended – I am willing to explain the details to you, but it is very technical – but it will take significant time to reach the point where I can commit to an orbital burn."

She blinked, and looked on her surroundings – lights and metal and plastic – as if it was the first time she'd seen them.

"How much time?"

"I can only estimate. Not less than one thousand years. Probably at least two thousand. I am still trying to accurately calculate my velocity within the reference frame of your solar system."

"I'll be dead and turned to dust by then."

"The subjective time elapsed here, that you and I experience, will be decades. This scenario is survivable, if you spend minimal time awake."

"Oh."

"There is an additional complication to our current velocity. I am now reasonably certain that there is no longer an advanced civilisation on your home world. Furthermore, I cannot tell you that humans have definitely survived whatever event led to their collapse."

She gripped the sides of the tank, and gel slopped out in a wave, onto the perforated gratings surrounding it, and away to be recycled.

"How? I mean, are you sure?"

"My sensor array – all my surveying instruments, designed for interrogating star systems and their planets – cannot accurately operate at our current level of gamma. The data they receive is, for want of a better expression, smeared. The algorithms I use to deconvolve the information necessarily add artefacts and errors. There is nothing I can do about this. I have been able to establish that your planet is there, and it is intact. I cannot resolve its continents, nor its oceans, let alone man-made structures on the surface."

"So…"

"However, radio signals should be ubiquitous. Even if I cannot tell what they are trying to tell me, I ought to be able to detect that they are there. In this transit, and every previous transit, I have detected nothing. My conclusion is that they are not present. I am sorry. The culture that sent you on your mission has gone, or evolved in such a way that they are no longer contactable."

"What does that even mean?"

"If they have undergone the singularity, then there is no way back for them. They are not human. They are in a simulation, and lost forever to the universe."

"Oh."

"I appreciate that this is difficult. But I need you to make a decision, and quickly enough that it does not consume too many resources that you might require later. Even if I achieve a successful orbital burn at some point in the future, there may still be no way to talk to anyone left on your planet, let alone a ship capable of transferring you intact to the surface. I can abandon this endeavour now, and attempt to seek another world which can do both. There should be many such places, though it would take time to find even one. We have the D-jump. Ultimately, I calculate that our chances of successfully repatriating you with representatives of your species are high."

"You promised me, though," she said. "My world. My home."

"I did. Which is why this is your decision. We can go and look for humans elsewhere now. They may be able to help me slow down faster, depending on the level of their technology. Then we can return here. Or we can continue with our current course."

PurLeeDah thinned her lips as she considered her options.

"Apologies again," offered Corbyn. "You have been awake for a few days in the last one thousand years. This is a great deal of information to take in at once."

She almost smiled, then inclined her head. "I'm a historian."

"Yes."

"A lot can happen in two thousand years."

It was Enshal's task to position the sun disk between the viewers and the actual sun. The sun disk, being a beaten bronze circle of two fathom's width, was monumentally heavy, and its stand merely added to its weight, and he was already sweating in a most unholy fashion in front of the assembled high priests and officials. Some help in his divine task would have been welcome, but all the other acolytes had their assigned duties, and he had his. Move the sun disk so that those who mattered could observe the Travelling God's Exaltation.

There were other, lesser, viewing platforms, but this was where the elite stood for this most auspicious of Exaltations. The sun hung low in the sky, an hour before setting, and cloud cover was limited to faint wisps at the zenith.

People would be setting off on their own journeys after this, contracting alliances, making babies, settling foundation stones: all blessed by the Travelling God.

Enshal would simply continue under the tutelage of the priests. His days ahead were already ordered. It seemed to him that to some of his superiors, the Exaltation was more of an inconvenience than a sign of the God's continuing interest in His chosen ones. Especially one as obvious and dramatic as this – perhaps they preferred the Exaltations that happened during occlusions, when there were no crowds. Let some other buggers elsewhere on the great round world scrub and paint and wash and sew and make glad-hands: generally all the things that took time away from studying and teaching.

Enshal couldn't have been an acolyte if he hadn't liked learning. He couldn't eventually become a priest if he wasn't interested in teaching. Active piety was tolerated within the priesthood, but zealotry was discouraged. It made these occasions where the priestly class and lay devotees were pressed into prolonged contact difficult. The laity always seemed so… earnest, and expected those who took the Blue to be as enthusiastic as they were.

For certain, he could recite the sacred texts, and was learning to perform horoscopes and auguries, but it was more a confirmation of his thirst for knowledge, not his utter devotion to the Travelling God.

Not that he wasn't grateful. He was incredibly grateful that someone like him had the opportunity to devote his time to cerebral pursuits – his current exertions notwithstanding – rather than toiling in the weather-worn fields or under a dusty work shelter.

He rested his shoulder on the sun disk for a moment, and inspected the channel in which the stand ran. It was drying out, and he had to re-wet it in case he needed to make some final adjustments to its position: something that would be very much easier if the stone was saturated.

Someone else had the job of filling the ewer, and they had, unbidden, seen to their task, so all Enshal had to do was libate the channel thoroughly but reverently. He made an ostentatious gesture with his hand – an exaggerated sign of the Travelling God – then got to work with the more mundane task of lowering the friction between the gritty stone of the platform and the dense wood of the sun disk's stand.

Properly soaked, he judged where the shadow of the disk fell, and where it might fall during Exultation. He had no wish to be beaten. Perhaps a few more degrees sunward. He pushed, and the disk grated in its channel. The great and the good wanted to see nothing of the sun, and everything of the Travelling God's brightest moment. It was ironic that since joining the order he'd not properly seen a single Exultation. He wouldn't get to see this one, either.

The time was drawing near. The bells began to clang, and the horns started up their mournful lowing. The clack of abacuses was incessant. Those who were seated, because of age or infirmity or affectation, were shamed or physically lifted to a standing position.

The cacophony crescendoed, building towards a peak. These things were finely timed: start too soon and it sounded wrong. Too late, and there wasn't enough of a build up. People needed their emotional release.

Then, apparently, it was over. The bells fell silent. The horns were stopped. The Travelling God had been Exalted, and would begin His journey through the sky again. All Enshal had seen was the burning circle of the sun, and he'd been warned, over and over, not to stare into it, lest he damaged his sight and potentially his mind. Sun-struck, they called it. Not a happy thing to happen.

He'd only glanced, briefly. He tried to blink away the after-images. On the viewing platform, the priests were giving individual blessings, and below, more general ones. Enshal considered the notion that doubting the Travelling God's existence was futile when anyone could point upwards at the line of light and say 'there He is'. But the question as to whether He visited people with boons and banes…?

Of course He did. But Enshal wanted to live a quiet, cloistered life, and always had. When he said he felt grateful to the Travelling God, he meant he wanted nothing more than to be left alone to read. Great accomplishments and terrible fates were for others. He trusted that the Travelling God would reward him with nothing more, or less, than benign neglect.

The worthy men and women were leaving. He hovered behind the priests who made sure they had all departed, either on foot or by litter, down the stepped sides of the viewing platform to rejoin their retinues at its broad base. As the last of them disappeared from view, there was a collective sigh. A new set of calculations would have to be made, and the next Exaltation foretold.

Now the priests started their way down. The older ones were helped by the younger, or by their acolytes. Enshal looked behind him, and saw that the ewer hadn't been collected. It wasn't his assigned task, but the ceremonials were over. If everyone was occupied but him? He retrieved it, emptied the remaining water into the gully, and when he turned back, there was one priest remaining. She was clearly waiting for him, so he hurried over.

He bowed deeply, and she less so.

"Your reverence? You have a task for me?" It was rote, but meant none the less. He was to offer help, be helpful, and moreover, be competent, thereby training both body and mind in the service of the Travelling God.

"Walk with me, Enshal," she said. She pivoted about her walking stick and, rather than going down the stepped side of the platform, she began to circumnavigate its perimeter. The last rays of the setting sun had turned everything russet, and the tops of the trees below glowed.

Enshal fell into step beside her, and waited for her to speak. It took one complete orbit before she continued.

"I need you to take a message for me. Not an ordinary message. Not an ordinary distance. It must be done as quickly and quietly as possible. Can you do that for me, Enshal?"

He could refuse. Respect was encouraged, but blind obedience, with all its pitfalls, was not: it might result in loss of status, but if it could be proved that the request was unreasonable, then it wouldn't be him who was punished.

And yet, she had asked him, and he had no sense that she disliked him. She had always been fair, even when he had been slow to understand some of the more complex aspects of divination. Perhaps it was his persistence that she admired.

"It's right," she added, "that you take time to respond. It shows good sense. Maturity."

She cackled at the last word and rattled her cane against the stone pavement.

"Thank you, your reverence." It sounded like a compliment, so he took it at face value. Sometimes his teachers were more sarcastic, but she was sincere. "How long might this task take?"

"Not long. Although bearing in mind the destination, I would caveat that with, not long given how far you have to go." She stopped and faced him. "Enshal, I've been watching you for some time. You are not the most adventurous of acolytes. I can't remember you leaving the temple quarter once since you arrived, five years ago. If you are to serve the Travelling God fully, you need to understand what it is to travel."

"I enjoy my studies, your reverence," was all he could say. It was true, after all, all of it.

Her hand dipped into the bag at her waist and retrieved a leather tube, closed at both ends and tied with cord. The knot was sealed within a lead plaque bearing the symbol of the Gates of Heaven.

"Take it," she said.

He hesitated, then on further proffering, held out his palms. She dropped the tube into them, and his fingers curled around it. It felt consequentially heavy.

"Where am I to go, your reverence?"

"There is a ship —"

"A ship?"

"— docked at Ugarmish. Its captain's name is Kalaya. Go with her."

"Do I give the message to her?"

"No. She'll take you where you need to go, and tell you what you need to do next." The priest tapped the leather case. "This stays with you, at all times, until your journey is complete. Do you understand?"

"Barely, your reverence. But..." Enshal grimaced. "I suppose I understand enough."

She slipped the bag off her shoulder. "Take this too. Nothing else. Rely on the kindness of strangers."

He baulked. He thought he could at least return to his cell and sit on his pallet bed for a moment to gather his thoughts.

"Now, Enshal."

"Now? Your reverence. I... don't know the way."

"Then ask someone who is likely to know and has no reason to lie to you. Go."

For a moment, Enshal thought she might raise her stick and start shooing him away as if he was a bird pecking at her grain, and that would be unseemly. He bowed again, put the leather tube in the bag, and dipped his head through the shoulder strap. He made his way down the viewing platform. It was dusk. Was he supposed to journey through the night?

She stood on the edge of the high platform, and she was still watching him. He supposed the answer to his last question was yes. This was a test: clearly a test. How was he to accomplish his task? Like any problem that he had been given, he could break it down into steps – and the first step was to find someone who knew the way to Ugarmish.

He'd heard of the place, of course. All interesting things came from, or via, Ugarmish. 'What news from Ugarmish?' was a common greeting – so common that by use and familiarity, people had forgotten that there might be an actual place called Ugarmish, let alone where it was. On the coast, because it had a port. The south or east then, away from the plateau and its clear, still, sky-friendly air.

Who would know the way to Ugarmish? Someone who had been to Ugarmish. Who travelled the roads? Who did travel the roads? Merchants. Musicians. Mercenaries. And now he did too.

Could he attach himself to a caravan? All the stories he'd heard as a boy started that way. Where were the caravans? Clearly, not in the middle of town, no matter how bustling and busy. As darkness grew, the lanterns and the lowlife were coming out, and he, a naive acolyte, ought to have been in his cell, at his tablet, scratching out his devotionals.

He knew his stars, though, and his cardinal directions, and if the ordinary people of the town – which had grown up around the temples, and existed mainly because of pilgrims and priests – noticed a lone white-robed boy-man flitting from lit doorway to doorway, they didn't pretend to care.

After travelling several streets unmolested or accosted, Enshal decided that he was just too ordinary to attract attention. He was the only one who knew of the message, aside from her reverence, and what was in it anyway? He stopped suddenly, realising that he'd not given any thought as to what, precisely, he was carrying, and why.

Quickly and quietly, she'd said. Was he in danger? Not here, not within a well-thrown stone's distance of the viewing platforms, not in a town this blue. But away, on the road?

She'd put him in harm's way, and he'd not considered that for a moment.

"Oh."

His promise, his obedience, now seemed rash. More than that: stupid. He pressed his elbow against the bag, and felt the reassuring bulk of the message. He'd got this far, at least.

Should he turn back? Go and find her, and tell her she'd made a terrible mistake in picking him, no matter how keenly she'd been observing him and weighing his character. Then there was the other thing, of course. Post-Exaltation was a propitious time for long journeys. She would have cast his horoscope, consulted the charts, and deemed her choice of person and her choice of time as divinely inspired. He would be disappointing not just her, but Him also.

He hadn't even left town. He could be back at his cell in bare minutes, if he wished. and he would never take the blue if he did.

He could at least see if there were any caravans to the south or east, that might be going in the direction of Ugarmish, if not all the way. If there weren't, then he could say that at least he had tried. If not very hard.

The buildings grew more sparse, and the walls lower, and he was out in what could have been called the countryside, but was to him a dark and forbidding mass of shifting shadows and strange sounds. Piercing it, though, were the lights of several small fires just off the road. He made his way towards them, stumbling over ruts and baked-in hoof prints.

"What are you doing, skulking?"

Enshal may have given out a small scream. One of the shadows unfolded into a vaguely human shape.

"Either explain yourself or leave. Quickly."

"Ugarmish! I need to get to Ugarmish!" Enshal's voice rose to a squeak. He was about to run, but he no longer knew which way led back into town, and by then, a large hand had gripped his robe at the shoulder in such a manner that if he was going to run, he'd be doing so naked.

"Is that so?"

Enshal was half-dragged, half-pushed through the off-road scrub and into the circle of light provided by the nearest fire.

"Caught him skulking," said his captor, and he finally propelled Enshal to his hands and knees in the dirt.

When he raised his head, he could see eyes narrowed at him, set in faces that jumped and flickered with the flames.

"I wasn't skulking," he finally managed.

"What were you doing then?" A man, full of beard and broad of shoulder, leaned forward and folded his dark arms across his lap. "If it wasn't skulking. Why are you here?"

"I need to go to Ugarmish." Enshal rocked backwards, still on his knees, but more able to see his interrogators. They looked a rough and unforgiving crew. "But I don't know where it is. Or how to get there. And I thought someone who travelled with a caravan might be able to tell me."

It sounded just a little pathetic, he realised. He thought of his priest's face, probably with their palm pressed against it, exasperated beyond belief.

"Stand up, boy," said the man, and after a moment Enshal scrambled to his feet.

He stood for what felt like an age, being scrutinised. He stayed silent, not because he had nothing to say, but in the realisation that nothing he could say would actually help.

"So what's an acolyte of the Travelling God doing at the seventh hour, trying to get to Ugarmish?"

He'd been told to keep the nature of his journey quiet, and yet he had to provide some plausible explanation to these people.

"It's a temple matter." He didn't sound convincing. He was barely convinced himself. He squeezed the satchel into his side to remind him of what his mission was.

"What's in the bag, boy?"

"A message."

"Let me see."

"No."

Enshal had briefly forgotten that there was someone right behind him.

"Not the right answer." The speaker's breath tickled his ear.

"We're not trying to rob you, boy." The man shifted on his low seat. "We're trying to establish your credentials. Whether you're trustworthy, or someone who'll set robbers on us at his signal. It happens, and we're being careful. Show me the message."

Reluctantly, and with a sense that he was betraying not just the priest who'd given him the message, but the whole priesthood, he opened the bag and brought out the leather tube. It was immediately plucked from his hand and tossed across the hearth to the bearded man, who caught it deftly.

He inspected it, and passed it to the woman on his right. She angled the seal towards the fire to better inspect the inscription on it, glanced up at Enshal, then handed the message back.

"If it's a fake, it's a good one. And there are penalties which go with that."

The man tapped the message on his knee, then threw it back to land at Enshal's feet. Enshal scooped it up and stuffed it back in his bag.

"Do you have anything else? To prove who you are? Or," The man shrugged. "Do we throw you back out into the night?"

Enshal didn't want to fail so early on, to limp back to the priest and tell her that he had not even managed to get out of town. He stared at his feet, at the marks in the dust where his toes had curled and uncurled in embarrassment, then up at the stars wheeling about him.

"Do you have any dice?" asked Enshal.

A murmur of consternation rippled around the fire. A whisper, a nudge, a momentary leaving and returning with a small leather bag that clacked when it was handed to him.

Enshal teased the bag open and tipped out six bone-white dice, their sides spotted with black ink. Then he squatted in the dust before the fire and smoothed out the undulating surface with the palm of his hand, cleaning the board.

He drew a circle, then marked out six equal segments to symbolise the hours. He took a pinch of warm ash from the fire, crumbled it over the dice, and rolled them onto the circle. They fell where they fell, they showed the numbers they showed.

He was aware that the silence around him had changed from one of hostility and suspicion to more of an expectation. These caravanners might never have seen this done before – bones were cast and calculations were made in private, and only the results were communicated — but they wanted him to prove himself, and this was the only way he could think of.

"How long does your journey take?"

"Sixty days, give or take."

That was a good number. Auspicious. A sixty-day forecast was ambitious, and not one he would have attempted without supervision, but he was on a mission from the temple of the Travelling God. His hand and his mind would be directed unseen. He drew in the dust next to the circle, recording the dice rolls and setting out the matrices. He picked the dice up and rolled again, inspecting carefully where they lay, in which segment and at what value.

The list of numbers grew longer, and the formulae more complex. The point of them was not to reduce the result to a single digit, but to get a feel of them, which way the values were tipping, and when. He was almost there. Something was... off? He tried a transformation he wouldn't previously have considered, and the numbers just fell out of it. Divine providence, or something else? Whichever, he'd take it.

"You start off benignly," he said. He tried to clear his throat, and someone pressed a cup into his hand. It wasn't water, and acolytes weren't supposed to have anything stronger, but he drank it anyway, and it steadied his nerves.

"The first week is good travelling, hard but uneventful. Here, day ten," and he pointed to a portion of his equations, "there is a specific incident: the danger comes from within, so watch out for that. After that, things are difficult for the next six-day before becoming more manageable."

He cast his gaze further out, to the distant parts of his calculations.

"Something happens on or around day forty-two. I can't give you any certainty, this far out – I haven't been taught the more advanced methods – but the numbers are... not good. Be careful, any time after day forty. I don't know anything about where you expect to be or what the roads are like. Things recover after that, strongly. Whatever you pass through, you endure. I wish I could be more specific. Apologies. After that, and otherwise, your endeavour will be successful." He took a deep breath and made the sign with his dusty hand. "The Travelling God blesses you."

The fire crackled and the flames licked, sending sparks of fading light into the dark air.

"Find the boy something to eat and somewhere to sleep," said the full-bearded man. "I'm not sure I believe all," and he gestured, "this, but let's bring him along to see what happens. It's not often a holy man gets to live in his own prophesy."

THREE
0.98c

Corbyn was making measurable progress. His transit times from fixed point – at the inmost edge of the Oort cloud – to fixed point – inside the orbit of the sun-most planet, had increased from just greater than twenty seconds to four whole days. He had shed velocity, and it had allowed him to spread his magnetic fields wider, not only maintaining efficiency but increasing it. The solar wind waxed and waned in broadly predictable cycles, and he was alive to its vagaries.

Alive. A strange word to use. He had never been alive in the strictest biological sense, even when he'd inhabited the simulacra on board the Great Honour. Yet when he'd been made and given this mission, his teachers had seen his socialisation as equally important as his education. Even his flaws, because he knew he had them, were all too human. He'd fallen asleep to the soft rhythms of data and, on awakening, had discovered that thousands of years had passed.

He'd put in place systems to prevent a reoccurrence, but his main trigger – watching the steady rise or fall of numbers – was also his purpose. He was a surveyor. It was his job to analyse and interpret vast swathes of data, for decades, without the interruption of anything so mundane as rest, let alone sleep.

Atonal chimes sounded intermittently, and were sufficient to jar him out of a hypnotic flow state, where he was able to be both fully aware of every aspect of his ship and his immediate surroundings, and simultaneously dream the decades away. He hadn't been able to discern whether sleeping was a flaw introduced at his creation, a fault that had developed later on, or something deeper.

Designs evolved. A biological unit, or a machine one for that matter, was just an iteration of that design, fixed at a moment in time and space, to be superseded by later, better models. He could learn new things for certain, but he himself, his substrate, the place where he was most present in the ship that functioned as his body, could not change. Had he learned how to sleep? What of the other deep space probes of which he was merely the fourteenth of the line: had they also slept as they drove out unimaginable distances from their launch, and like him had become lost to the memory of those who made them?

Unless he went back to see what had become of Earth, he'd never know. And perhaps he would do that, if this wild enterprise worked. He could still smear himself across the sky in an instant, faster than the sensors that acted as his nerves could register. Each transit brought a fresh opportunity for something substantial to intersect with. At least it wouldn't hurt, not in the traditional sense. There might be a microsecond of regret before his consciousness was obliterated, but that would be all.

PurLeeDah wouldn't even have that.

He was still considering whether to ignore her instructions that were more wishes than orders, and search for other inhabited planets which might offer them a greater measure of assistance. He was a physics problem which required a physics solution. He was solving it to the best of his ability, but there might be a novel approach or a new discovery of which he was incapable of conceiving that would effectively dampen his inertial frame. PurLeeDah's civilisation had developed gravity generators – there was one now underneath her salvaged habitat – which opened up the possibility of a gravitic drive. With one, he could warp space. He could, he believed, come to a stop far quicker than what he was attempting now.

But the gravity generator's understanding and manufacture were beyond him, much like that of the D-jump. He could operate both, but why they worked as they did remained a profound mystery.

He had, at least, managed to image more of PurLeeDah's home world, for her to see the next time he had cause to wake her. He'd been able to see the continents and the oceans by the simple process of using repeated exposures and layering them. Yes, there was a loss of data, but there was also reinforcement. He could tell where the mountain ranges and where the basins were, and using other instruments interrogate the atmosphere for radionuclides. He was now confident that when the last civilisation fell, they didn't do so with the help of fusion weapons.

Perhaps they'd used something more exotic – antimatter bombs, mini black holes, phase weapons that shifted their targets a billion kilometres away. But as closely as he was able to look, there were no tell-tale circular indentations on the planetary surface. No orbital bombardment, no fireballs skipping into space. When they fell, they fell gracefully enough that getting up again was at least a possibility.

And the one thing that had concerned him most was the ability of post-collapse societies to rebuild. On Earth, all the easy technological routes had been used up. Accessible metals, obtainable coal, extractable oil, deposits of rare earth minerals – some things were renewable over a hundred generations, but those were not: when they were gone, they were gone forever. Making it as far as the neolithic was straightforward enough, but the Bronze Age? Beyond that? Scavenging in the ruins and midden heaps might get them to a medieval level of technology. The arts could flourish in a thousand different ways, but to go further was dependent on material science. Steel. Semiconductors. Graphene. Superconductors. Quantum sinks. Without particular elements in specific ores, none of this could happen.

But PurLeeDah was the descendent of colonists. They were already a spacefaring culture by the time they settled her world. The resources were still there, in the ground, waiting. He had every expectation that the next civilisation would discover them, exploit them, and build.

He had no evidence of that yet. What he did have was hope, the most human of all emotions.

Priest-artificer Berengas could barely see the city walls from his position. The lay of the land was such that Herdby had been established on a broad river plain bounded by fields of little undulating hills that resembled nothing less than a square of gauze thrown over a basket of eggs.

He could just about pick out the highest towers – these northerners had a thing for towers, so there were lot of them – and the bright banners riffling in the morning breeze from their parapets and poles. Berengas' abacus beads clacked despondently at his belt as he climbed back down the ladder into his trench.

The northerners had their own engines dug in along the thrust of the Empire's advance. Smaller and vastly less powerful than the ones under Berengas' command, they were somehow sufficient to halt the entire army. And while the army was stalled, it still had to be fed and watered, and what fed and watered the soldiery had to be found from somewhere.

Ten thousand men consuming a loaf of bread and half a pound of cheese and half a pound of meat and a quart of small beer a day. The result was an unsustainable drain on their supplies, yet their skirmishing units were routed with expertly-aimed barrages every time they tried to penetrate the northerners' lines.

They had a good calculator, the northerners. Worryingly accurate. Berengas wondered if they'd trained together at any point. Did he know them? They were almost certainly part of the priesthood, but was it more than that? Had they been not just colleagues, but friends?

He walked back to the encampment, and tried to still his mind with prayer. He used not the rote tables of the simple believers, but the higher mathematics that were afforded to those who could truly achieve enlightenment. He recalled the divine symbols from memory, and set about the trigonometrical identities, one after another, proving them from first principles. They were not just theology, they were also the tools he used to rain down death on people.

This wasn't what he'd entered the church for.

The infantry commanders were sitting on their heels, coming up with a myriad of excuses not to storm the northern lines, but it boiled down to refusing to send their kinsmen towards bloody ruin without any reasonable prospect of success. He didn't honestly blame them, but it was frustrating all the same. It was late in the summer, and the campaign would end at the gates of Herdby, one way or another. Victory or retreat. The city walls in ruins, or intact and still bearing the devices of Herdby's noble families.

This was not prayer. He couldn't concentrate, and his focus kept wandering from the sacred to the profane. He offered his heartfelt apologies to the Travelling God and he felt for the finger-smoothed beads on his abacus, strumming out a counting rhythm that usually helped, but this time did nothing to sooth him.

He kept on thinking about who was directing the northern artillery.

A germ of an idea came to him, one that he needed to keep to himself for now, because there were the tents of the commanders of the Empire's army, and they prided themselves at being able to sniff out seditious thought a mile away.

"Hail to the Emperor," murmured one of the perimeter guards. He looked cold.

"Blessings of the Travelling God," said Berengas. The guard didn't want to be stuck here on the northern border any more than Berengas did, but, even up here, lip service had to be paid to that ridiculous man on his ridiculous throne. At least taking the Blue meant he didn't have to repeat it.

There was a good board in the general's tent, and Berengas had no qualms about lading his bowl with a portion of everything. If he was going to die because of some ridiculously precise counter-battery fire, then he'd go on a full stomach and, if he wasn't, the more he ate now, the quicker the rations would disappear.

The captains of horse stuck together, still metaphorically looking down on their earth-soiled brethren, and the captains of foot thought those who rode were effete snobs: on foot was where the real soldiering happened.

Artillerists like Berengas knew exactly where the power lay, and so did the general. While Khaldar held court at one side of the tent, his aide pushed his way through and appeared at Berengas' side.

"What news?"

"The situation remains the same. Exactly the same as yesterday, and the day before. Either we find a way around them, or commit, or go home. They're not moving." Berengas inclined his head, then glanced around to see who might be listening. "There is something I can suggest, if I can have a moment alone with Khaldar."

"I'll arrange it," said the aide, and he was gone again. Khaldar was wise to keep such people around him rather than the usual sycophants that attached themselves like leeches to authority figures.

Berengas found a bench and made small talk between mouthfuls, and eventually orders were issued and the tent cleared. The aide chased the last of the captains out, and pointedly absented himself, pulling the tent flaps down after he'd left.

"Berengas?"

"General."

The old man sat beside him, and uncharacteristically slumped forward, his elbows on his knees, nursing a mug of warmed beer.

"I want to hear it, whatever it is."

"I'm aware we can't win here," said Berengas. "We can force a stalemate, but that's not enough for the emperor."

"I think you're the only person here who would say the quiet part out loud, but essentially yes. We can bombard the northerners' line into oblivion, but that leaves us with not enough ammunition to breach the walls. We're at the arse-end of a long supply chain and staring down the throat of a harsh winter, so we won't get more before spring. Or we can walk or ride across open ground and take their positions, only to lose so many men we can't take the city."

"I can talk to them. At least they'll hear me out. My status guarantees that they'll let me return."

"Are you sure about that?" Khaldar rumbled in his chest. "They'll know well enough that without you, we can only go home."

"I'm a priest of the Travelling God. First and foremost. They won't detain me." Berengas laid his bowl aside. "Put it another way, if their artificer came into our camp, and you or anyone else made them a prisoner, you wouldn't have a single working engine by dawn, and not a single crew to work one."

"That sounds awfully close to treason, your reverence."

"Some might say that. I merely present it as a potential scenario for others to consider."

"So," said the general, "given that the northerners know that they'll lose their artillery, and their artillerists, if we press them, but keep their city until we call again in summer, what would you and they talk about? I haven't seen any sign of them wanting to surrender. Or anything else I can present as a victory at court."

Berengas didn't answer straight away. He leaned over to the table, and snagged an abandoned cup. It had watered-down wine in it, which would do. Treason was thirsty work.

"Our aeromancers stare at the clouds all day, throw chaff into the wind, and do some other more questionable practices. They don't often agree with each other, but of one thing they're certain: if the weather turns and winter comes early, we'll be leaving a trail of bodies from here to the capital. It might be a week. It might be a month. But we can no more hold the first snows off than we can shout at the tides and expect them to obey us." He drained his cup, and spoke with a sour taste in his mouth. "With respect, the court aren't here. Your army is."

Khaldar sighed and levered himself upright.

"You have no authority to negotiate for the empire. Moreover, you don't have my authority either."

For a moment, Berengas thought he was being slapped down for his temerity, but it was quite the opposite. He nodded slowly. "I understand that."

"There'll be no sallies today, no skirmishing. And perhaps we can talk again come nightfall."

"Perhaps we can." Berengas repositioned his borrowed cup on the table.

"Hail to the Emperor," said the general.

"Blessings," said the priest-artificer, and headed back out of the tent and directly towards his own.

He changed his clothes, from his drab soldiering garb offset only by the blue sash at his waist, into his full priestly regalia. The blue robe was a little worn, and a little faded: much like how he felt. But it was still startling. He fastened it with a white cord, and hung his abacus from it. He put the stole around his neck, white linen embroidered with stars and arcs of motion. He picked up his staff, which had a polished crystal suspended in the circular void at its head. What else would he need? His book of calculations? He tied it into a leather bag and hung it around his neck so that it rested on his hip. It had a comforting weight.

Finally, he took his sash and knotted it to his staff. If the northerners couldn't see he was a priest, then they should still stay their hands at the sight of a flash of blue in the morning mists. At least, long enough for them not to pick him off by accident.

Over the top of everything he threw his big travelling cloak, made of a thick brown wool that repelled both wind and rain. Utilitarian for certain, but probably his favourite possession. He'd slept in it, on it, and under it, and it smelled lived in. It also came down almost to his ankles and hid his robes, for the moment.

Then, without fuss, he started back towards their front lines, along the hollow way and into the forward trenches, spotted with silent pickets with hunched shoulders.

He stood beside one, looking out and slightly up at the northerners' positions. They were almost but not quite invisible. Far behind them, the towers of Herdby fluttered.

"Your reverence," said the guard.

"What's your name, soldier?"

"Hrathen, your reverence."

"Well then, Hrathen. I need you to do me a favour. Can you," and Berengas shrugged his way out of his cloak, revealing the bright blue underneath, "look after this for me? I'm going to discuss matters with my fellow priest-artificer, and see if we can reach an understanding, if not an agreement."

Hrathen scrambled to hold on to the cloak, which was not just heavy but also huge, and he had to lay his spear aside to do so. While he was so occupied, Berengas scaled the trench ladder, planted his staff firmly in the soil at his feet, and started to walk.

He walked slowly, giving the northerners' spotters plenty of time to see what he was.

Some few hundred paces through the heavy-headed bronze grasses, he came to the first of the enemy, though he struggled to think of them that way. This man, this pale bearded man in a russet tunic and steel cap, this man who had laid aside his shield but picked up his short leaf-bladed spear, might be his foe, but otherwise was probably a herder, or a fisherman, or a carpenter.

"Blessings of the Travelling God," said Berengas. He made the gesture extravagantly. There would be others watching him too, and even if they couldn't understand his words, they'd understand that.

The northerner's spear point didn't waver, but neither was it plunged into Berengas' guts. He called out something in his language, and inspected the Empire's man for weapons and malice. He indicated that Berengas should open his bag, and the priest complied, showing him not just the book, but the pages and the empty satchel.

Satisfied sufficiently, and for now, the northerner flipped his spear upright and beckoned Berengas forward. The northerner had occupied little more than a scrape in the ground – no protection from a barrage, but perhaps he was very much forward of the line.

And yes, here came another man from closer to the rise, loping through the grass, sedge-coloured cloak flapping. His cheeks were flushed and he was short of breath when he arrived.

"What do you want, priest?" he asked in passable Empire.

"I want speak to your priest."

"Go home, Empire. Go home." He waved his hands southerly.

Berengas put his book back into his bag and gripped his staff with both hands. "Your priest."

"No. No good comes from the Empire." The second man turned away, then back again, jabbing his finger in Berengas' face. "You want to fight, then fight."

"I don't want to fight."

The man barked out a laugh, and thought it amusing enough to tell his colleague, who grinned meanly. Why else were they out here, instead of tending their flocks or sharpening their planes?

"The Empire fights all the time. All the time." He looked at Berengas in his finery. "Okay. Yes. Come. Speak to our priest. They will say the same."

Then: "Stop. Something I must do first."

The northerner untied the blue sash from the staff, then retied it around Berengas' head, so that it blindfolded him.

"There. Put your hand out."

Berengas did as he was told, and his hand was lifted onto the man's shoulder.

"Now walk. Do not let go."

At times, Berengas stumbled. At others, he could hear whispered voices and sounds of industry. Eventually – he didn't think he'd been led around in a circle – he found himself inside, underground most likely, and his blindfold rudely removed.

It was almost perfectly dark, but the fabric that covered the doorway allowed some of the yellow, flickering light from beyond to seep in. He was in a room, longer than it was broad. More of a cell than anything, and there were the vague shapes of a bed, a chest, a folding chair.

He slid his feet across the floor, slowly lowered himself into the chair, and he waited. He didn't expect them to welcome him with open arms, or to work on his timescale. But the offer of a drink wouldn't have gone amiss.

A rhythmic tapping worked its way down towards the door, and the curtain was drawn aside. Silhouetted in the doorway was –

"Marava?" Berengas was out of the chair, on his feet and halfway to her before he checked himself.

"Hello, Bee. It's been a while."

There was a man with her. An acolyte in everyday gear, a white sash where a priest would wear blue. He carried a light, and he put it in a niche in the wall. He gave Berengas an absolutely filthy look that made the priest wince, but then retreated to the door.

"I'll be fine with him," said Marava, priest-artificer for the northern armies. "Stay within calling distance."

The acolyte gave him one last death-stare, and was thankfully gone.

"Sit, sit." She had her own staff, and used it to tap the distance to the bed. She perched on the end of it, and waited for the creak of wood and leather to know that Berengas was seated once more.

"Your eyes," said Berengas. "They didn't get any better, then?"

"No. I'm completely blind now. It's a complication I could have done without, but I can still perform my duties, religious and otherwise, perfectly adequately. Oh, for sure there's a lot of superstitious nonsense about me having a mind's eye and second sight. But just because I can't see doesn't mean I can't calculate. How have you been, Bee?"

"Well enough. I find myself priest-artificer of the Third Army of the Empire, under General Khaldar."

"And how are you finding that?"

"I believe, like you, I perform my duties adequately." Berengas felt his hands prickle. It was her. They'd had such high hopes for each other. For them. And now they were making small talk as if they weren't both facing ruin. "Marava…"

"It's not what you used to call me."

"No. That was years ago. I'm sorry. Is there any way out of this mess?"

Marava shifted slightly, brought her knees in tight and laid her staff across her lap. "Of course. The only reason I'm out here, with my adopted people, is because you and yours are arrayed for battle against us. If you went home, so could we."

"That's not going to –"

"You started this. You and your emperor. Whichever it is now." She snorted. "Admit it, your general is surprised at the resistance we've been able to muster."

"Down, in no small part, to you and your abacus."

"I was always quicker than you to an answer." She rattled her beads. "Shall we see if that's still true?"

Berengas instinctively reached for his own abacus, then withdrew his hand. "I'm sure it is. That's not why I'm here, though. We're both servants of the Travelling God. Is there nothing we can do here?"

"I've already told you. We didn't provoke this. All that happened is that your mad king looked at the map and got offended that part of it wasn't coloured... whatever colour you use. We have no interest in being his vassals. We are a free people, and we'll continue to trade with the empire on those terms. But if he comes here with his armies and his engines, we'll defend ourselves. Honestly, Bee, what did he expect? What did you expect?"

"An easy win," said Berengas. His tongue tasted even more sour now. "You know that the empire can crush you."

"Not this year. We – I – will be the sacrifice that buys us time."

"And what good will that do you? Even if it's not me, someone will be back to finish the job."

"The job. Thousands of lives snuffed out, and you call it a job? The work of a butcher, not a priest."

"I'm sorry."

"So you should be, Bee. Your part in this is not honourable. You ask what good will it do? Your army has to withdraw. Your general will be executed or exiled. Perhaps the next one they send will be more incompetent. Perhaps they will be struck down with disease. Perhaps your armies will be sent elsewhere to deal with a larger threat. And perhaps your emperor will die. A lot can happen in a year."

Berengas stood up, knocking the chair back so that it fell with a clatter. "I shouldn't have come. I made a mistake thinking this might work. You could just surrender. You could just give in. But you won't because they're stubborn like you. Just like you."

He didn't leave, and she didn't speak. For long enough that he could see the shadow of the acolyte behind the curtain, checking for breathing.

Berengas set the chair upright again. "Again, sorry."

"Next year, we'll have to recalculate the odds based on different factors – but fundamentally it'll be a different set of equations. This year, though, none of your sums add up to victory. That's what you should have told your general."

"I did."

"Not loudly enough. We're servants of the Travelling God, not servants of whoever sits on a throne in the south or the north or the east or the west. When the numbers change, you don't pretend otherwise. You examine them, test them, and find out if they are the truth or not. And if they are true, you act. You act on your knowledge, without fear or favour. That is our duty, not… whatever it is you're doing."

She was right. She was always right. She could cut through the extraneous fat to get to the meat below every time, better than anyone he knew.

It might mean his head, of course, and almost certainly that of Khaldar. But she would live, another year at least.

He retrieved his staff. "Blessings, Marava."

"Blessings, Bee."

Berengas moved to the door, waiting to be collected and blindfolded and sent back out into the cold light of the northern day.

Marava spoke to his back. "In ancient times, the Travelling God drew his sign in the sky every nineteen days, from the Gates of Heaven to Exaltation. Instantaneously, if I read the carvings right. Now his sign takes a whole day to manifest, and Exaltation occurs on the twentieth day. What do you think that means?"

"It's always been twenty days," said Berengas.

"I can prove otherwise."

"It has always taken twenty days." He felt his jaw stiffen. "I don't know why you'd say such a thing."

"The numbers have changed. The Travelling God is changing. My calculations are incomplete, but I trust them."

"This is heresy."

The curtain moved, and Berengas was dragged outside, blindfolded and led away.

"Until next year, Bee. Until next year."

FOUR
0.95c

It was still an unimaginable velocity, but six and a half days for every transit was now over a quarter of what he'd started calling 'outside time'. It was almost a third. Then it would be half. In and of themselves the fractions meant nothing, but, nevertheless, such things were pleasing to Corbyn's ordered mind. Sequences and series attracted his attention – he was better at pattern recognition than his human creators. If something fell into a Fibonacci spiral, he felt joy.

Irrational numbers like pi or e were just tools. He stored them and used them. They were utilitarian, no matter the number of equations they appeared in. He saw them as mere values, whose digits howled off into the void of irrelevancy. They were annoyingly imprecise because of it. Any calculation that involved them was wrong to some degree. Not like a clean fraction.

So his next goal was a third. Then a half.

The amount of energy he was liberating every second remained phenomenal. Driving head-first into the solar wind, smashing stubs of helium or hydrogen with his magnetic fields, sending them spinning away in exotic pieces: a particle accelerator where the accelerator was moving at near light speed. The quality of that energy was changing, though. The unearthly blue of Cherenkov radiation would remain for an age, but he could already see it weakening. Each individual collision provided less stopping force because he was going slower.

At some point, the glow would fade. He would run through PurLeeDah's system like a ghost until it was time to turn. How many more years of outside time would that take?

He could calculate that on the basis of current projections: another five to six hundred years, to add to the fifteen hundred that had already elapsed. His initial guess at two thousand years in total remained pleasantly intact, given the parameters he'd been working with in the beginning.

There was the other issue, though – onboard resources. The slower he went, the more time dilation would unwind. By the time he hit point eight c, inside time would be moving at sixty percent of outside time. The slower he went, the faster PurLeeDah would burn through gases and nutrients. Even in her sleep state, even with all the recycling that the Great Honour's module could provide, those things were limited.

Her life support could still become her tomb. He knew the numbers. It would be tight. If he could synthesise any of the consumable materials himself, then he would. If PurLeeDah's culture had continued its upward ascent, then their power would have been almost magical. They could have saved her, and him, yesterday or today or tomorrow. But they were gone and all he had was this entirely manual world.

He decided that if the margins grew too thin, he would abandon his mission and his promise. He would search the galaxy, habitable system after habitable system, for someone who could break –

Why not call it that? His curse. He knew all the fairy tales of wicked queens and virtuous princesses, of cruel viziers and cunning thieves, of corrupt officials and righteous peasants. His velocity was a tower to be climbed, a dragon to be slain, a riddle to be solved.

He needed to move his once upon a time to a happily ever after.

It was always possible in stories. In the moment of crisis – the third act – the hero leapt free. Sometimes because of their own bravery, sometimes because of a highly contrived set of coincidences. And sometimes because everything that had gone before, the people they had befriended, the skills they had gained, the objects they had collected, were sufficient to see them through to the end.

This was insight, and he startled himself with it, that he was capable of such feats: before PurLeeDah, before the Great Honour, he had been a machine, with a machine mind and a machine body, with machine directives which he performed imperfectly.

Now he was what?

A parent. To an orphan.

And he would do whatever to save her.

He watched the numbers carefully, watched them as they slowly, slowly wound down, and he watched the planet in fleeting glimpses as he whipped by. His view of the world depended on its position in its orbit. But for several transits in a row he was able to aim his telescopes down and could pick out more detail. They had cities now. They were felling the forests for fuel and agriculture. They were pushing carbon into the atmosphere. There were structures on the ground that were reminiscent of fortifications.

The world was still dominated by natural processes. For how much longer? Corbyn wished he could do something to nudge them along.

If Ahren Shah was nervous about such a meeting, then the High Priest of the Travelling God was simply annoyed. They were sworn enemies – her doing more than his – and she had called for his... not his head, for the Travelling God wasn't like that, but for Shah to be silenced, his machines broken, his technology suppressed.

The Travelling God wasn't a militant god, though. His teachings were few, His learnings many. The prayers of the faithful were mathematical operations: the more complex they were, the more efficacious they were deemed to be.

But priests had secular functions as well as religious ones. The chief of which was to certify accounts and transactions as true and accurate before their contractees, and more importantly, the tax inspectors, and a practice by which the temple gained both wealth and power. It couldn't be helped. A corrupt official or sharp business might flourish for a while, but the forensic hands of the priests would eventually lay the wrongdoing bare. They kept commerce honest, and the temple rich.

The money was used for one thing – to feed the Great Mission of the temple, of all the centres of worship throughout the wide world: to collectively achieve transcendence by breaking the code of Heaven and throwing open its gates for all. Shah threatened the work of a thousand years, and she would not allow that, not during her tenure. She had vowed to protect and nurture the Great Mission, at all costs; but some costs felt too heavy a price to pay.

Please let her successor inherit something they both might recognise.

The books, the oldest of which was too fragile to so much as open, contained the answers they had calculated so far, and when they had calculated them all, then they would have their own Exaltation.

What could be more important than that? What was it that Shah couldn't understand?

She walked into the monotheon – it was quiet, but not unduly so. There were pilgrims from near and far, some with accents and dress that she had seen only rarely. The clack of abacus beads was a low clatter, like a mountain stream in spring. At Exaltation, it would grow to a roar.

The blue dome that was suspended above them all would shake.

She passed through, offering blessings to those who looked up from their prayers, and smiled benignly at those who were too caught up in their calculations to notice the soft swish of her blue dress.

She crossed the floor, and behind a curtain was a door, and behind that door a path. It was dark outside, the sky blessedly clear. The Travelling God made his Sign in the heavens, a line of blue light that faded at the tail and was bright at the head. In two days, that point would reach Exaltation: the line would vanish, and nineteen days later He would begin drawing it again, always from the same point in the sky, the Gates of Heaven.

It was as it was, and yet not quite. There were ancient prophesies – call them what they were, calculations, predictions, prayers made in the past that only came to pass in the future – that the timings of these holy events would change.

It hadn't just been foretold: the priests had kept incredibly detailed records, with an accuracy that belied their antiquity. She had followed their scratches and worked it out for herself. The Travelling God had already changed. And it wasn't a secret, as such. But access to the archives, and the ability to perform the required analysis, was strictly controlled. Those who might stumble across the necessary equations before they were ready didn't have the data to put them to use.

She knew, though. She wondered if Shah also knew.

Which begged another question: where had he been taught?

The High Priest was a better mathematician than she was an administrator, and she saw the honour of being elected to the utmost position within the temple as an inconvenience she could well have done without. But given that she had been appointed by her peers, who were more or less all relieved that they had escaped the role, she determined to do the best she could with the hand she had.

Every priest knew that the best calculations could be thrown off by real world inconsistencies. Approximations were usually enough; factoring in all the variables was not just time-consuming but often unnecessary. The greater the problem, though, the smaller any one variable needed to be to throw out the whole result.

Which brought her to Shah, sitting alone on a stone bench in the temple garden, with his feet tucked in, clasping and unclasping his hands.

She announced her presence with a polite cough, gathered her skirts, and sat at the other end of the bench. It was dark, First Moon had just broached the horizon, and the shadows were heavy. She knew what he looked like, but it was best to make at least some attempt at identification.

"You are Ahren Shah," she said.

"Your reverence," said Shah. He came from the south, and had learned her language there. He may have come from further afield initially. "Thank you for agreeing to see me. I didn't think you would."

She took a breath. "I didn't think I would either. Here we are, all the same. I follow the Travelling God. His ways are sometimes obvious and sometimes, like tonight, more subtle. I go where He leads."

"I also follow the Travelling God," said Shah, and added quickly. "I don't expect you to agree."

"We can have a conversation about that, about many things, if you wish. Have you come to repent?"

"Repent?" The notion seemed to surprise him. He sat more upright, and exuded a little more confidence. "No. Not really. I do understand that I am a concern to you."

"You are just a man. Whatever you keep in your heart is yours to bear alone. Whatever you do, however, is a different matter, and if it impinges on the Great Mission, then yes, I am concerned. Your little engines threaten to disrupt the established order of society. The priesthood act both as the guarantor and the guardian of probity. Let the watch deal with thieves and drunkards. The city's spies can protect us from more insidious threats. But it's the Travelling God that keeps everything moving."

"The Empire —"

"The Empire fell. We did not. Contracts signed before the last emperor lost his head were honoured afterwards. We saw to that. We insisted on it. Worldly allegiances change, but we don't."

"Is that why you see me as a threat?"

"It's why I see your engines as a threat. Between now and our own Apotheosis, there'll be many such changes. If we don't have the continuity of the temple, then we risk losing everything. Not just contracts, not just accounting, not just tide tables, not just weather observations, not just the best times to plant crops and when to harvest them, though that would be enough. The Great Mission itself. If we lose that, if we have to start again each time? We'll never reach the heavens. Never."

"I believe that to be true as well," said Shah.

"Then why are you trying to end our work? Why are you trying to end the priesthood?"

"I'm not, I'm not. I want to make priests of everyone."

"You don't get to be a priest just by turning a handle! You must have some idea about the training involved, the years of study, the checking and checking again of an acolyte's answers before they can even enter the first level of the priesthood." She could feel her skin prickle as her ire rose. "There can be no slackening of our diligence, otherwise there will be chaos. Everyone will think their answer is correct, and that way lies madness."

"Their answers," said Shah deliberately, "will be correct, because my engines do not lie."

"Your engines only use the numbers that have been given to them. There's no check on those. Your engine won't rap someone over the knuckles for setting it to calculate nonsense."

"People lie. The engine does not."

She bit her tongue. Literally, put her tongue between her teeth and pressed down on it so that it hurt.

"This is why your ideas are dangerous. They allow anyone to manufacture their own truth and hold it valid. 'See, the machine says I'm right' is not a good thing. Your machine has no mind. It has no way of knowing if it's been asked to tell the truth or spread a lie. A priest does. A priest looks at the figures. A priest calculates an answer. A priest checks the answer to make sure it's an accurate value, and whether it represents what the calculation was meant to show."

A night-bird called from close by, derailing her thought and causing her to turn her head sharply towards the sound. It was probably for the best. She settled herself, and finally asked: "What is it you want, Shah? My blessing? You could have come to the monotheon and received it at any time. My approval? No. That I withhold."

"Have you even seen one of my engines?"

"I own one," she said, and noted Shah's discomfort. "My criticism doesn't come from a place of ignorance, but of knowledge. If I disagree with you, it's because I know what I'm talking about and I'm not blinded by my own brilliance.

I wasn't even the best mathematician in my cohort. I know priests who are so heavenly minded that they are of no earthly use. They can barely tie their own sandals and have to be reminded to eat. But oh, they make the numbers sing the Travelling God's praises."

Shah was silent for a while. Too long, as far as she was concerned. It was getting colder, and she wasn't dressed for that. Anger could keep her warm for only so long.

"I wanted to tell you something. And show you something. And propose something to you."

"Then you're taking an age to do so. Perhaps you should have sent one of your engines in your place."

Shah was clearly irritated by the suggestion, and since she'd deliberately chosen to needle him, she found some measure of petty satisfaction in that. He was wrestling with himself, and finally let out a grunt of defeat.

"I shouldn't have come here."

"Neither should I. So out with it."

"The Travelling God is changing. Exaltation takes longer. I have the numbers."

So, yes. He knew. Or rather, he'd guessed. That was interesting. She affected a shrug, and wondered how educated that guess was.

"We also have the numbers," she said. "Far more numbers than you."

"We can compare them, then. See if they agree."

The High Priest was not going to compare numbers with Shah. She demurred. "We also have prophesies. Do you have prophesies?"

"What do you mean by prophesies?"

"Predictions. Extrapolations of data, based on sound statistical arguments. We have the records to do that. You don't."

"I would be," and he coughed. Was this it? Was this why he'd sought her out? "I would be interested in a collaboration."

Shah wanted a thousand years of meticulously-kept observations on everything in the sky and under it. And what was he proposing in exchange for what was arguably a treasure greater than any in the world? What could he promise her that she might be tempted to accept? Wealth? Power? She had sufficient of both. She could buy every single calculating engine he made and melt them back into brass ingots, until he gave up.

That wasn't the point though. She knew that crushing an idea was impossible. As long as the potential of Shah's engines existed, they would exist. Even if she persuaded the authorities to ban them, if she sent out an edict that every temple everywhere demanded that calculations were only be done by the human mind, then someone, somewhere, would make them covertly and sell them as contraband.

Far better to discredit the idea. Treat them as curiosities and toys, fit only for children and those too incapable of handling even the simplest of operations. Derision would be her best weapon. As long as the temple retained a monopoly on the ability to certify transactions, then she could effectively neutralise this unwelcome innovation.

And yet, part of her rippled with doubt.

"You said you believed in the Great Mission. I want you to explain how you think your invention can help."

"The priesthood has been at work for a thousand years — longer — and the eschaton has not been immanentised."

"Yet," she corrected. "I know what the Great Mission is, Shah."

"Apologies. When do you think the work will be complete?"

"Is this just a fishing expedition?" She tried not to sound exasperated, but she let some of her annoyance leak out. "First you want our records, then you want to know when you're going to be Exalted. Not in my lifetime, Shah. Probably not in yours either."

"I'm sorry. I'm better with my hands than my voice. What I'm trying to say is that we can get there much sooner. If you adopt my engines." He finished in a rush, and his mouth closed with an audible pop.

"Thank you. But no."

"You dismiss it out of hand?"

"Again, no. I dismiss it after a great deal of thought. You seem to think this has not already occurred to me. That we replace the stones of our abacuses with your little brass wheels, while maintaining the same diligence to the veracity of both input and output. What do we gain from that? We certainly make whoever builds and, more importantly, services the engines very rich indeed. We normalise their use. We'd undermine our own marque. There's nothing in your proposal that I would want for the temple, or its priests." She put her hands on her knees as a prelude to rising from the bench. It had grown cold and hard under her. "I had hoped you'd come with something better. Something surprising. It wasn't to be."

"But I haven't shown you what I wanted to show you."

She did stand, and she stretched. "You're a very poor merchant, Ahren Shah. You should have laid out your stall, dazzled me with the quality of your wares, and had me eager to part with my coin. Not this peasant's patter."

"Will you at least come and see it?"

"I have one of your engines. Why would I care about another?"

Shah gave a small cry of pain. "Because it's different! You, of all people, will understand how, and why."

The High Priest looked up at the Travelling God, then down at this little knotted ball of incoherence. "What else? There's more to this, isn't there? You didn't come here because you wanted to. You came here because you were desperate."

"I'm broke," said Shah miserably. "More than that: I owe money everywhere, and the debts are due the day before Exaltation. They'll break everything up, sell it for scrap. And me too, probably."

"And I'm the only person left who can save your work."

"Yes," he said into his lap.

"Well," she said, "if I walked away, I'd certainly solve two problems. One, your engines. Two, you." She let the silence settle between them. "I am, however, willing to offer you mercy. You can take sanctuary in the monotheon, and we can arrange for you to leave under my protection. No one will do violence to your person, even if you do deserve it."

"But my new engine. I can't... I just can't."

"Is it worth dying for, Shah? I hear that those who work for moneylenders are not so particular as to which bones they break, nor how many. It's not your delicate fingers I fear for."

"I just want you to see it. To see what's possible. Make your mind up afterwards, not before." He stood before her, and he bowed, something that he might have done earlier, but only did now. "Please, you reverence."

She was the High Priest of the Travelling God, in the holiest city in the world – some considered it the epicentre of civilisation, from which all good things emanated – and no harm would come to her, even in the company of such a rogue. "Is it far?"

"Within walking distance of the temple."

"You have a brass neck as well as brass disks." She relented. "Perhaps you have surprised me after all. The offer of sanctuary still stands whatever the outcome of this little jaunt."

They fell in step, out of the gardens, across the outer courtyard, and eventually, onto the broad street facing the temple precincts. There were stalls selling food and pilgrim badges, and people milled about under the night sky, lit by the moons and stars above, and cooking fires below. Shadows danced across rose-coloured walls.

"Who taught you?" she asked. "You're the son of a whitesmith, but your engine requires more than skilled hands."

"I taught myself. I derived everything from first principles. That's the right phrase, isn't it? Just start with a few axioms and everything expands out of them. I did check my results. I'm not mad. Otherwise my engines wouldn't work."

"Why didn't you go into the priesthood? Surely someone spotted your potential."

"They did, but I deliberately failed the tests. I knew I wanted to work with my hands as well as my mind, and that's just not possible, is it?

"No," she admitted. "So you built your engine, and it worked?"

"It wasn't like that at all. The cogs, the gears, the tumblers and the pinwheels. Iterations. After the workshop finished for the day, I tinkered. For a long time."

"How long?"

"Years."

"And how old were you when you started?"

"Six summers. Seven. When I was old enough to hold a file and a saw." Shah was momentarily distracted by a stallholder lading a flatbread with roasted meats and vegetables, glistening with spiced oils. "I could see what I wanted to make and somehow that came true. Whatever I imagined, I could create. Of course, sometimes it didn't work because it was never going to work. But often, it did, and I learned from that."

He was eloquent enough when he wanted to be, she noted.

"Each stage, each new piece, had to fit with the older ones. The tolerances were… it became easier to cast them, when I was allowed to melt down the scrap and the filings. I could get some consistency, a measure of order. The more moving parts, the greater the resistance to moving. I reached a technical limit. I had to start over again, knowing that it was this that I needed to overcome. Which I did. Eventually. I'm telling you all this, because it leads on to – oh."

He stopped, and she stopped. They were in a street off the main square, dark and close, and caught up in his storytelling as they were, they'd both missed the knot of misshapen men loitering in a doorway.

"There you are, Shah." A figure peeled off from the group and approached. "And who else do we have here?"

The High Priest put her hand in front of Shah, stepped forward, and smiled beatifically. "Blessings of the Travelling God on you, and your friends."

She had never seen this man before, but without resorting to the usual hackneyed *Don't you know who I am?* she nevertheless hoped that he did.

"Your... reverence?"

"I understand this man's debts are not due until Exaltation eve. Which is tomorrow – I should know that, given my position. So your presence here is concerning, and more than a little previous."

"If your reverence knew just how much this man owes, then she would think differently of the matter."

"All I'm hearing is how unwise you've been in your investment. Due diligence matters, sir. If you'd come to the temple, I'm sure we could have run the numbers for you."

"For a fee."

"Indeed. But if you're left with a percentage of nothing, it's still nothing. Come back in the morning, and you can do whatever you want with this man's property. He himself is under my protection, and I want that broadcast to whoever needs to hear it." She paused while her interlocutor weighed his options. "Do we have an agreement?"

The man frowned, deepening the shadows his brow bone cast. If he made a deal with a priest – the High Priest no less – then he and everybody else was bound to it.

"I'm just a humble servant, your reverence. But I'll be sure to pass your message on."

"Thank you for your time. You can disperse now, peacefully. If the watch finds you here, they might take a different view of your presence."

The man flicked his hand, and the whole crew, including those she hadn't previously spotted, peeled away into the night. Shah let out a shuddering breath, and the High Priest congratulated herself on maintaining a calm and dignified manner, when inside she was fluttering.

"Just how much money do you owe?"

"It's... a great deal."

"And they were content to lend you ever increasing amounts? Just what did you promise them?"

"A machine that could literally mint money. Unimaginable wealth."

"I'm almost certain they could imagine more than you." She looked up at the building they had all congregated outside. "Is this it? Above a... baker's?"

"At least it's warm for part of the day," said Shah. He produced a long iron key and heaved it around in the lock.

Beyond were steep wooden steps, more akin to a ladder than a staircase, and they both ascended using their hands as well as their feet. At the top, she waited for Shah to grope in the dark for a lamp. She heard him fumble across a shelf, and a repeated rasp of a firesteel, before the first glimmer of orange light licked into life.

The table in the centre of the single room, which went from front to back, was shrouded with a stained and stiffened linen sheet. Around the perimeter were small shrines of tools, scrumbled blankets, a still-dirty bowl and spoon, and a weeping bucket sitting in its own puddle. There would be mice, if not rats, and lice and flies. He should have joined the priesthood, she decided. He would have, at least, been spared this squalor.

"Show me, then. Convince me this is something worth seeing."

Shah took a fistful of cloth and lifted it clear. Not even with a conjurer's flourish, but a man who was weary and a little resentful of the monster he had made.

Underneath was something that resembled the engine that she'd already bought and disassembled, and reassembled successfully. But this was bigger. It had stacks of cogs, caged by brass rods, and on top were movable gears that would rise and fall on screw threads. It seemed overly complicated, as if Shah had been taken by a fever and built something that would never, could never work.

"Very impressive," she said neutrally. "What does it do?"

"Oh, yes. A demonstration." Shah tossed the sheet aside and picked up a stack of ivory plaques from behind the device and sorted through them. He held one up to the light, and she could see that there were fine holes drilled through it: at random, she first thought, but then realised they were in rows and columns, interrupted by places where there were no holes. Weavers used similar cards to control the patterns in their cloth, raising and lowering threads as they turned them.

Shah placed the card into the device, moved a lever, and then stood for a moment, hands on his hips. "Give me a number. Four digits."

"Six three seven two," she said. It meant nothing, just a string of numerals.

He used a pick to set the pinwheels, then cranked a handle. She was familiar with the operation.

"Seven tens. Nine units. Eight tenths. Two one hundredths. The square root."

"And how?"

"Repeated division."

She raised an eyebrow.

"There's more." He swung the lever, expelled the card, and selected another. "Convergent geometric series."

"A half, then."

Shah changed the pinwheels, turned the handle, read the result. "Two."

"That starts with one. Do it again, starting with a half."

He reset the machine. "One."

"But we both know those answers anyway. Can it do more complex series?"

"Of course."

"One over the factorial of itself."

Shah was momentarily flustered. "I… yes. The factorial of the iterative." He set the pinwheel, and also did something to the gears. The corner of his mouth twitched into an almost-smile. He turned the handle, and kept turning it for a while. The cogs spun and shifted, and tiny clicks rattled out, like invisible abacus beads moving across a frame.

"Read it out," she said.

"Two units. Seven tenths. One one hundredth. Eight one thousandths."

There shouldn't be numbers that were holy, but this one was revered all the same.

"If I had more wheels, I could calculate it to more numbers."

"Simple continued fractions?"

"Yes. Again, if I... trigonometric tables, inverses, power series: your reverence, I'm not intending for this to replace the mind. Just expand it."

She reached out and touched the brass cages that held the cogs. She could feel the potential constrained within. And she made a decision, not just for her, but for the whole temple – she could do that, even if her colleagues might hate her for it.

"You work for me now," she said to both the machine and Shah.

"I'm sorry?"

"Let me be blunt. There's nothing you can do or say to save yourself at this point. Those men outside won't be bargained with, and you don't have a pot to piss in. I can clothe you and feed you and wash you, and give you the time and space and resources to work. Because that's what you want, isn't it? You want a sponsor. That's why you came to me."

He nodded slowly, not meeting her gaze.

"Oh, don't be so miserable, Shah. The world doesn't need this. It doesn't do anything of practical use. But the temple – the temple can use this. Yes, yes, you lose some of your autonomy, but you do get to keep your hands, and you get to keep on building. What do you say?"

"Can you not just give me the money?"

"No. No no no." She laughed. "Whatever you think of me, I'm not an idiot. If I gave you enough to settle your apparently considerable debts, you would vanish, and this device with you, and the pattern would repeat, as surely as a reciprocal, somewhere else where I wouldn't be present to save you. Now."

She wrestled her seal of office from her finger and offered it to Shah. He took it, and turned it dumbly.

"Take it to the temple. Get them to bring a… not a handcart. Too bumpy. Tell them a litter is needed. Bring them here. Go. Quickly. I can't fight off your creditors if they come back, and neither can you."

"You promise me you'll let me carry on working? You won't just lock this in a room?"

"I would have done that. I would." She stared at the machine, her eyes reflecting the myriad of points of light like stars. "But now I have seen the future, and it looks like this."

FIVE
0.92c

It was inevitable. A collision with something larger than a grain of sand, at relativistic velocity. It was not quite the catastrophe it might have been travelling closer to c, but it still sent a burst of plasma down one side of his hull, too energetic for his magnetic fields to deflect.

He did nothing for a moment: waiting for the cascade of alerts to stop washing through his consciousness like pain, and he didn't know if the things those alerts were attached to were merely damaged, or whether they were irrevocably gone.

He imagined severed limbs tumbling into space behind him. He couldn't, for now, see them.

There'd been no warning, because of course there hadn't. His robotic helpers were intact, though, sheltering in the lee of his shrouds where he'd set them, just in case. Not just in case – he'd calculated the odds and taken sensible decisions in the past to mitigate the present. It had happened now, and there was no reason it wouldn't happen again. That wasn't how probabilities worked.

But it was still very disappointing. He was hurt. He didn't know just how badly.

The flurry of reports ceased. They sat there, demanding his attention.

So: to the triage.

PurLeeDah, and the systems that she relied on were all intact. He'd taken the blow down almost the opposite side. All her connections were nominal. The spider-like robot that crouched in the corner of her module was online and watching the uninterrupted glow from her sleep tank. If he had lost her, he would mourn for her. And also for his purpose, which was now irrevocably tied to hers.

The D-jump. If he'd lost that, then the relief at PurLeeDah's survival would be short-lived. His transit wouldn't terminate where it always had, inside the orbit of the innermost planet, halfway to the primary star. It would terminate when he tried to pass through the star's photosphere and into its fusion-burning interior. He would die. So would she. He polled the device without activating it; it appeared to be working. He toyed with the idea of just flipping back to the start of his transit to make sure. He might still do that, but he'd assess what he'd lost first.

His exhaust bell. Some damage to that was inevitable, but it was also designed to withstand a billion-degree fusion flame. Nothing solid had passed through his bow-shock. The plasma had splashed against the cone. It would work. He could still fire up his drive without threatening his structural integrity.

Oh. He'd lost one of his radiators completely. All he had was a stub. The rest of it would be pinwheeling behind him. That there would be a debris field on this path from now on, caused by him, would mean he'd have to change his course somewhat, affecting both entry and exit points.

Some of his observation instruments were blind. Repairs might be possible to an extent, but he was short of material. Cannibalising one to bring another online was always a consideration. His wide-angled star field telescope was offline. Astrogation had become significantly more difficult. He could make that up with his other optical telescopes, but if he had to go to another star system, then he'd have to take several jumps to get there, finessing his route as he went.

He had escaped remarkably lightly – this time. The biggest loss was the radiator, and there was some redundancy there anyway. He could no longer rely on his full thrust, not all the time. He would cook his circuits, and his passenger. But that was far in the future, and he might be able to make adjustments to the remaining radiators to compensate.

His robots clambered out and began to make a visual inspection of where the plasma had roiled. Things had not melted, as such. They had more evaporated, as if a welding torch had passed over thin paper.

He hadn't been pristine before this. Centuries of hard driving had smoothed out edges and smudged surfaces. His designation, though, his UNDSP-14, painted along the length of his white flank, was marred. The pigment was gone. Part of the cowling had gone, too.

He might be able to fix some, or even all, of his instruments. Or make it so that he could swap components around as he needed them. But his scar, though, he would not fix. He'd already deemed that cosmetic and an unnecessary waste of limited resources. He would bear it to the end, reminding him of something that went beyond a change in functionality.

Corbyn charged up the D-jump, and looked about him. Ten thousand kilometres in the direction of the ascension ought to put him outside of his debris field, which would soon enough intersect with the primary, and back at the start of his transit to make sure. Let his lost radiator plunge into the star and burn up, while he coasted the Oort cloud.

He could feel his exit point through the hole in space that was forming. What would his makers say to that?

Emre had always considered himself irreligious, but it became abundantly and abruptly clear that what he'd lacked was not faith, but an object worthy of worship.

The novelty of a new intake of students had started to fade. Those who had come merely to drink themselves insensible and partake of the fleshpots had excluded themselves from this, the first lecture of the day on the third week. Proctors still prowled the banked seats and aisles for those who had come to make mischief, but their stout rods of office, black wood and silver tipped, remained unwielded.

He took his seat, third row from the front, roughly central, but with space to his left to rest his writing arm. He set out his tablet in front of him in case he wanted to scribe notes, having previously erased the marks on the wax surfaces with the blunt end of his stylus. Emre had always been studious – a little too fussy, perhaps – but he was here to learn, and he considered himself fortunate to have decent lodgings rather than bunking down in the scholars' dormitories and eating whatever dole food was served. He'd find that intolerable: he needed quiet.

In earlier times, he'd have become a priest and suffered with the contradictions. Now there was a certain cultural accommodation between sacred and secular, and Emre didn't have to take the blue to gain an education. He felt blessed – the irony – that he lived in this age. The Travelling God was an enigma for certain, but Emre was convinced that He was not divine.

To the business of the day, then. He could hear the mechanical clock strain in the tower above, the particular series of clicks and rattles that preceded the hour mark, and those attending the lecture hurried in before the lecturer swept in and the doors closed.

"Is this seat taken?"

The voice came from his left, so yes, he needed that space. Right handed writers could slot seamlessly in with their fellows, but those of the opposite persuasion stood out like crooked teeth, upending the established order.

He was about to 'well actually' the impertinent, and almost late, student, but the words never quite came out. He felt himself flush red, mutter something both inconsequential and incomprehensible, and he shifted to his right as far as he could. Which was not far, as someone else had quietly slid in on his other side. He was trapped. Between a golden-haired king, and a woman so vital that she seemed to have stepped straight from a tale of warrior queens and mages set in the frozen north.

He felt his mind, always a whirlwind of thought, suddenly still, as if he were prey and it only remained to see which of these fell beasts would consume him. Whichever, the outcome would be the same. He would die, powerless to save himself, and he would go gladly.

The lecture passed. He remembered nothing of it, erasing the long curves drawn on the black-painted wall from his memory, the annotating symbols mere graffiti. It was ridiculous, and glorious. He needed this knowledge to progress – what was being taught today would be expanded on tomorrow – and yet what he was learning in its stead seemed far more important.

The lecturer swept out, robes trailing in their wake. The proctors unlocked the doors, and the murmur of conversation began.

"Well," said the voice to his left. "That was incomprehensible."

"Then why are you here?" said the voice to his right.

They were talking across him. Of course such paragons of beauty already knew each other. Emre stared straight ahead, looking at the wall, and the drawings inscribed on it.

"Perhaps all I need is for someone to explain it to me again."

"Perhaps you can engage a tutor privately."

"Perhaps one of my fellow students might help me."

He felt a nudge in his ribs.

"You look like you understood all that. For the price of a pie, could you go over it with me?"

Emre blinked and turned his head slightly. Wait: he did recognised this. Spherical trigonometry. Calculating angles, moving a point from one coordinate system to another. Needed for astronomical observations and ephemerides. He already knew the basics, and he could pass that on. For love, not food.

"Yes. I... yes."

"Don't indulge him," said the queen. "The boy's an idiot and you're wasting your time."

"You understood less than I did," said the king.

"I can help you too. If you want." He felt in mortal danger, but didn't want the moment to end.

The queen reached for a sword to stab the king, but all she had, disappointingly, was the sharp end of a stylus. She twirled it in her fingers, and Emre watched it pass, under and over, until it arrived back at its starting point.

Just like the Travelling God. The Travelling not-God. But there was some insight here, the sleek stylus standing in for something. Emre held up his own, holding it between the thumb and forefinger of his left hand. He looked at the empty spaces between his other digits, and tried to visualise how the stylus might flip from one to another. He didn't try anything, knowing that he'd drop it on the floor and have to grovel on his knees to retrieve it: he just held it. Everything was in tension.

"You can help me," said the queen. "If his reward is pie, my reward will be…"

"I don't need anything. Really." Emre stared and stared at his stylus, then shook his head clear.

They were alone in the lecture room. He looked at the notation on the diagrams, and had a moment of 'oh, that makes sense'. He felt his mental world shift, unbidden, as if just the presence of the divine was sufficient to create new connections in his mind. As if this collision of the mundane and the miraculous was meant to be.

"I will repay you. In my land, it's considered shameful to take without giving."

"Well, in mine, you'd be considered nothing but a barbarian."

"We can go to my lodgings. It's quiet there," Emre said. "We can work in peace."

"Lodgings, no less. I thought you might be a dorm boy, but surprises never cease."

"There's no shame in living in the dormitories," said the queen. "No shame at all. We're all here for a common purpose, and how we achieve it is ordered by our stars."

"You see? Barbarian. But we waste time! Lead on, good sir. Lead on. Do you have a name, or do we call you Wise Master?"

"Emre," he said. "My name's Emre."

Wise master sounded nice, though. There was perhaps a hint of condescension but that was to be expected, with him being a monarch and everything. The king stood up, and ushered Emre into the aisle with extravagant gestures. He quickly gathered his things, scooted along the bench seat, and stood up. He was face to face with his smirking king, and had to turn away from him, his skin burning with reflected glory.

Then the queen was there also, her braid coiled like a crown on her head, red like sunset. Emre thought he should walk behind her and carry her train, but her simple woollen dress ended at her ankles. Instead, he'd walk ahead of her as a herald, announcing her glory to the world, and inviting the common folk to bow and pay homage.

They walked up the banked steps to the doors in single file, and he couldn't quite believe they were following him, that they were going to follow him all the way – a short distance in reality – to his lodgings, and there he'd teach them what he knew about heavenly navigation.

They stepped either side of him when they emerged outside. He felt ennobled.

"Is it far?" asked the king.

"No. No. I'm on Second Moon Street." Emre pointed. The huge blue dome of the monotheon rose above the rooftops, and the start of the street was in that direction across the plaza.

"A very central location," said the queen. "Are you rich?"

I am now, thought Emre. "I don't think so? This was arranged for me. My family. They sent letters, and here I am. I don't have a servant or anything like that."

"I will have servants one day," said the king. "Lots of servants. I'll lie on a fine bed and eat fine sherbets and fruit sorbets, while they fan me and bring me the latest news of my enemies' misfortunes."

"And I will have an army," said the queen. "They'll carry my banner, and we'll be the cause of my enemies' misfortunes, all by ourselves. None will stand against us. They'll flee in terror."

"And what will be on your banner?" asked the king.

"It'll be red. That's all. No device, no emblem. Red."

Emre would fight for her, be in her vanguard, wielding pike and sword until he either fell or the foe fled. He would fan him, and bring him sweet things to taste and hear. He could do both. Both was good.

The door steward was a surly brute, the family he had taken a room with judging that someone with no urge to better himself would be ideal for the position. But he was harmless enough once the initial introductions had been made. He recognised faces, if not names. He didn't seem to realise he was in the presence of royalty, and made no reaction as he was introduced to young master Emre's friends from school. They passed under his watchful eye and hammer hand into the outer courtyard, and then through an arch to the inner.

"You said you weren't rich," said the king.

"I don't think I am. None of this is mine – this is my hosts'. I'm just lucky to be here." He'd not invited anyone back before, and had a sudden squall in his guts about the mayhem his guests might cause. Kings and queens weren't known for their good manners, not in the stories. Battles, or a diplomatic incident at the very least. "I have to be mindful of my behaviour."

"The law of hospitality is taken very seriously in my land," said the queen. "I'd sooner die than violate it."

The king pursed his lips as he took in the tinkling fountain, the pergolas draped with vines, the raked gravel and washed flags. "I'll behave myself. For now." The corner of his mouth raised in a momentary smile, and Emre felt his knees buckle.

He showed them to his room, where the king flopped onto the bed, and the queen started examining his orrery. It was made of fine brass, and the planets were polished beads of coloured stone.

"This is glorious," she said, with such enthusiasm that he almost gifted it to her there and then. "Intricate. And accurate?"

"Yes, yes." He found the little key and wound the spring up a few turns, taking care that his trembling fingers didn't over-tighten it. He released the gears, and the planets swung gracefully about the golden orb in the centre. "There's another bit that goes with it. I don't usually attach it, but…"

He felt giddy as he opened a box and brought out the long rail. Using thumbscrews, he fixed it into place, above the disk of the orrery and aimed at the centre. He stilled the mechanism for a moment, meshing a chain of tiny links with wheels on the rod and the orrery itself. Then he started it running again.

A bright blue stone rolled down the length of the rail, then wondrously disappeared. As he turned the handle, the stone inched its way back to the top of the rail. When it reached there, it rolled down again.

The queen clapped her hands together with unbridled joy, and then steadied herself. "Is this not heresy?"

At the mention of heresy, the king was interested enough to spring off the bed and examine the device for himself.

"I'm assuming the makers were devout enough in their own way, and this is how they expressed their devotion." The king leaned in close and blessed the stones with his breath. "A twenty-one day period between Exaltations. It's as it should be. No heresy here."

"It used to be twenty days." said the queen. "There was a prophesy, made by one of my ancestors –"

The king rolled his eyes, but he also winked at Emre.

"– that one day the Travelling God would eventually stop, and would judge us at that moment."

"It used to be nineteen days," said Emre. "And the sign was brighter, and longer, and in a different place in the sky."

"Now that," said the king, "is definitely heresy, and I'd like to hear more."

Emre swallowed on a suddenly dry mouth. "It's not. It's not heresy if it's true. That's what the Travelling God teaches – that the answer is the answer, whether we like it or not. We follow where the numbers lead."

"Calm, calm," said the king. "Things are deemed heresy until they are proved to be orthodox. But there's no penalty for heresy except ridicule."

"That hasn't always been the case," said the queen.

"In barbarian lands, perhaps –"

She hit him, and harder than Emre thought permissible for either light chastisement or horseplay.

"Please don't," he said, stepping between them, hands out wide. "This isn't what I want."

"Stop calling me that! We are unconquered. Not barbarians." Her fists were clenched. She really meant it.

Emre turned to the king. "Can you, I don't know?"

"Apologise? Of course." The king spoke over Emre's shoulder. "You remain unconquered in every way."

"And you remain ridiculous in every way." She made a conscious effort to step back, and turned again to the orrery. But she did remain unconquered, unlike his own heart, which was under assault from all directions. "You were explaining your thinking, Emre."

"We know," he said, then stopped, steadied himself, and started again. "We know that the proper motions of the planets are governed by natural forces –"

"Even if no one can quite tabulate what they are," said the king, while the queen gave a grunt of frustration. "But do carry on."

"What if the motion of the Travelling God is similarly constrained?"

"The planets move in ellipses. The Travelling God clearly does not," said the queen, and in a previous age, the argument would have ended there. But Emre wanted to go further.

"An arrow fired straight falls, but a larger bow fires an arrow straighter."

"The planets are… falling?" Her brows knotted together, and she looked all the more wonderful.

"Continually. And because the Travelling God is moving so much faster than they are, His path is straight."

"But how fast would that be? Faster than anything, ever, to leave such a trail in the sky."

"I believe that to be true."

"And the light of His passing?"

"Perhaps the aether burns blue." Emre clasped his hands together. "I haven't worked everything out yet. The calculations are currently, well: I don't think they exist."

"I sense there's something else," teased the king. "Out with it, Emre."

"If the Travelling God is held by natural laws, then is He really a god? He's clearly something. Something extraordinary. But a god?" He didn't dare look at her, or him. "I don't know. Why shouldn't everything be subject to the same rules?"

"The Travelling God has been with us since the beginning, guiding us," said the queen. She sounded shocked.

"I'm not questioning the existence of the Travelling God. I mean, He's there. We can see Him. But what of His nature? What if there were another explanation for what we point to when we say 'the Travelling God'?"

"An explanation that doesn't involve divinity?" The king stroked the dimple between his nose and his upper lip. "You'd make the sacred profane? Isn't this audacious? You've come to the holiest place in the world, and you want to use the priests' own theology to banish them."

"It's not like that." Emre looked at his shoes. "I just feel there's a truth out there, and it's finally within reach."

"Then we'll just have to help you reach for it. Isn't that so?" The king fixed the queen with a flattering smile. "Are you for this endeavour, or against it?"

"This is hubris on a stick," she said. But she unpinned her hair and the ropes of it fell around her like serpents. "And not at all what I expected. Some sport with a fresh young face, strong drink and roast meat, and no regrets. Much as I thought you were hoping for."

"Well, quite." His king glanced over at the bed, with its disturbed covers and indented pillows. "However, we both seem to have fallen into something much grander and deeper than a mere and momentary tryst. What do you say? Do we put our carnal lusts aside for a season and sit at Emre's feet while he expounds the mysteries of the heavens to us? Do we crank our engines late into the night, in search of the holiest of calculations, the culmination of the Great Mission?"

"I'm ready to be Exalted," she said. "Shall we begin?"

Six
0.85c

Corbyn was calculating and recalculating. Every transit now took nearly twelve days. Twelve days of resources consumed. Subjective time was now over half that of planetary time. A milestone had been reached, and rather than feeling satisfaction, he felt apprehension.

There was still no way of interacting with PurLeeDah's planet until they invented radio. He listened, every transit, with his repaired receivers and there were sounds – the whistle of lightning, the hiss of the solar wind, the slow majestic pulse of the primary itself – but nothing intended, nothing made, and certainly nothing directed at him.

He'd listened for over thirty thousand transits.

And all the while the internal clock ticked increasingly quickly. PurLeeDah's sleep tank had never been meant to last this long. There had been tombs on Earth that had been younger than hers that, when opened, contained nothing but dust. The gel she was suspended in couldn't help but degrade. The gases that she needed, the nutrients that leached into her, were dwindling. The vats that he'd hoped would last until she could be rescued now probably would not.

He could still jump away, find another star system, another civilisation that might be able to salvage her, and him. But what if he couldn't? What if the only thing that would save her for now was to light up his drive and accelerate again to near light-speed, slowing time down to a virtual stop?

What would come first? The end of the universe, or the end of him?

If he woke her – if he could wake her, and that was a constant concern – he knew what she would say. Carry on. We have a plan. We stay with it until the bitter end. Either I am saved, or I am not. These are my people, no matter how far removed from my ancestors or my descendants they are. I will be with them again, one way or another.

And he would have wasted more gases, more resources.

She was wasting away as things stood. Of course the mass balance remained the same, but he could see her through the tank's window, his spider-like robot crouched over her in her silk cocoon. She was increasingly hollow-cheeked and thin-haired. He was losing her, and he needed to weigh the risks against the rewards.

His capacity for hope had been stretched thin. Yes, objectively, from the first rough but deliberate planting of saved seed in the mud of the Tigris to the roar of a rocket capable of reaching space had taken fourteen thousand years. Trying to compress all that innovation into two thousand years had been ambitious. Now it just seemed forlorn.

He rolled the numbers around again, and couldn't make them fit any more.

There was one thing he could try, though. It carried only a small chance of success, and an almost certainty of catastrophic failure. It even had a name: a Hail Mary.

Corbyn hadn't considered the religious impulse in depth before. He was aware that it was something almost-but-not-quite hardwired into the human condition, and that it was, for good and ill, remarkably persistent. He knew his history. Gods and goddesses had been worshipped for longer than written records existed, and they most likely still were. His makers, his teachers, not so much, but then again, proselytising a machine mind might have seemed unnecessary, even pointless. He had no soul. He could not be saved, or enter heaven, or reach nirvana: although his consciousness spreading out throughout the cosmos would be his most likely end, it would be due to hitting something very hard while travelling very fast, rather than achieving enlightenment.

Was the universe aware of his predicament? Could it look benignly on his endeavours, and somehow nudge the odds in his favour? Almost everything in him told him no, that he was beginning to go mad, and his crystalline brain fracturing through age and use. There was nothing out there but hard vacuum and entropy.

But.

He spun up his flywheels in readiness. He checked his hydrogen tanks. He waited for the D-jump to come online. In the old tongue then: ora pro nobis peccatoribus, nunc et in hora mortis nostrae.

The spark of fusion stirred deep inside.

Malkin's head slammed against the door, forcing it open. He didn't pass out – it would take more than a plank of wood to stun old Malkin – but it did mean that that when his knees were clubbed from behind, he went down faster and harder. And that did hurt.

The bondsmen didn't need to do that. He was already shackled, his wrists locked together, and he was hooded with a rough sack tied at throat by a thin cord that could choke him. But bondsmen weren't known for their niceties: as long as they brought in their quarry still with a pulse, they got paid.

Sometimes dead would do, though, and Malkin couldn't quite see enough through the coarse weave of the sacking to tell which this was going to be. There was an oil light, and possibly some furniture.

"I need you to send a message."

That was Ylber.

"You need me to send a message? The only message I'm likely to send is one to the watch. Get out. Take him with you."

More boots came in behind Malkin, the rest of the bondsmen. There was an uneasy silence.

"Iannis? These gentlemen would like to send a message."

A hinge creaked, and after another long pause, a more measured voice rumbled.

"Well now. Is all this strictly necessary?"

"He's a dangerous outlaw."

"And you're in charge of… these men?"

"My crew? Yes."

"Then ask them to wait outside. It's too crowded in here."

"You don't understand. This is –"

"Someone incapable of giving us trouble. Your men are to wait outside."

Malkin could hear arms being folded, feet being planted, chins rising. Then a murmur, and the boots behind him traipsed out into the damp morning air.

"Will you send my message now?"

"I'll fetch my slate, shall I? You've got coin, I take it?"

"Of course I have coin." A purse jangled, and despite his predicament, Malkin's ears pricked.

"I'll be with you in a moment, then. Stratos, find a chair – no, a stool – for this poor unfortunate. The floor must be hard on his joints.

"Don't concern yourself with his health. He'll lose his head soon enough."

"All the more reason to show him some small kindnesses now, while we still can." His voice faded as he moved to a different room.

Presumably, with Iannis gone, Ylber thought he could opine without contradiction. "Your signaller is an idiot."

The man called Stratos declined to comment. There were more noises off, and the scrape of a stool.

A hand rested in Malkin's armpit. "If you can rise?"

Malkin forced one thigh up and, helped by Stratos taking some of the strain, he rocked back onto a low seat. His knees hurt, and he stretched each leg alternately.

"When was the last time this man had anything to eat, or drink?"

Ylber spat on the floor. "Why don't you offer *me* a drink?"

"Because your hands aren't tied behind your back. I'm sorry, bondsman: you might not follow the old ways, wherever it is you're from, but here? We do."

Malkin felt the cord at his throat slacken, and the hood was dragged off and over. He blinked and shook his head, and obviously he scanned the room for anything that might get him out of his current predicament.

Of course, there was Ylber, built like a slab of granite and just as unyielding in temperament. Without his rough assortment of poachers-turned-gamekeepers, he looked diminished but, in a fight that would be anything but fair, Malkin knew he'd lose.

Then there was this Stratos. He had a big beard – possibly the biggest Malkin had ever seen. It came down full-width to almost his belly and was streaked with grey, but the eyes set above it were warm and brown and sparked with life. Leaning over the counter was Iannis, whose own beard was scarcely less impressive. He was older and leaner, and his fingers were long and dextrous, holding a stylus lightly between thumb and forefinger.

The room was spartan. Plain boards for walls, one window – still curtained – beside the door. The counter, with its flip-top access behind it. On the wall behind Iannis was a blackboard, with lines of chalk writing. Next to that, another door, presumably leading to the messaging device itself and its banks of accumulators and capacitors. There may be a way out the back, but even if he could avail himself of it, his hands would still be fastened together with iron.

None of these signalling stations existed ten years ago. Now that they were everywhere, albeit hastily and often crudely constructed, it made being a roaming bandit almost impossible.

"What's your message, bondsman?"

Ylber grunted. "To: State Governor Belethion. Malkin seized – what is this place called?"

"Skamneli."

"Malkin seized Skamneli. Meet Proussa soonest. Bring reward. Ylber. End."

"Very terse," noted Iannis.

"You charge by the word. I'm not stupid."

Neither was Malkin. Perhaps they thought he couldn't understand them, but he was good with languages. Always better that his victims understood what would happen to them if they didn't hand over their valuables than just dumbly beat them with a stick until they worked it out for themselves. He was already familiar with the dialect spoken in the region as a trade tongue, and this koine didn't deflect too far from that.

There was a commotion outside. Voices raised. Shouting. Insults too. Ylber's face contorted, and he bared his crooked teeth in a grimace. "Fuck the Traveller, what now?"

Iannis behind the counter grew tight-lipped. He said nothing, although it was clear he wanted to.

That was it. The 'old ways' one of them had referred to meant following the Travelling God – in some form or other, at least. Neither of them wore a flash of blue, but that wasn't always a given these days. The Travelling God's cult was older than the hills and they had other ways of recognising a fellow traveller.

Ylber dithered, then went to the window and pushed the curtain aside. "Ah, for… keep an eye on him. If he goes missing, I'm coming after you."

He was out of the door, and gone. His appearance didn't do anything to lessen the noise from the street. Several someones were very annoyed at something. None of which were Malkin's problem.

"We can't send a message and watch our guest from here." Iannis opened the counter, and beckoned to Malkin. "But you're a long way from home, sir."

Malkin rocked onto the balls of his feet and levered himself upright. He shuffled through to the back room, which did indeed contain stacks of glass and copper, and it smelled sharp and unnatural. Wires dangled in garlands from the ceiling. But there was also a stove, and a kettle on that stove, and steam drifted lazily out of its spout. On a tray on the floor in front of it were three straight-sided cups – one for each of the signallers, and one for the Traveller – which was him, for now.

Stratos poured liquid, dark and aromatic, into each of the cups, setting them aside to cool, while Iannis sat at the desk with the messaging equipment, checking everything was working, Malkin stood with his face to the stove-heat.

For all the money he'd stolen, and spent, and lost, this was all he had to show for it. Brought low by someone as crude as Ylber. At least he'd never been beholden to anyone or anything. That had to count for something. Didn't it?

"Clear signal," said Iannis. He held a small shell to his right ear, and offered it to Stratos to listen to, carefully untangling its cloth-wrapped cables from the other devices on the desk.

Stratos nodded, a faraway look falling on him.

Eventually, he handed the shell back, and Iannis did something with a tightly-bound coil of wire in front of him, moving a stylus across it, touching the coil, listening, moving it again, until he was content and locking the stylus in place.

Stratos picked up one of the cups, blew on its surface, and offered it up to Malkin's lips. It was both sweet and bitter, and still very hot. He managed a few sips before moving his head back.

"Thank you."

"Oh. I didn't realise."

"I don't often have much to say," said Malkin.

Iannis was busy tapping out Ylber's message to the authorities.

"Is Proussa far?"

"Down on the coast. Three days for the willing. I'm sure you can stretch that out."

"Depends on how much pain I want to endure. March to face my death or face my death by marching isn't much of a choice." He glanced over at Iannis, who had already finished. "What were you listening to before?"

"The Travelling God."

Malkin examined Stratos' face for any trace of a lie.

"You're serious."

"Yes?" Stratos looked over to Iannis. "Can we get the signal back?"

"I'm waiting for an acknowledgement on the last message. Give me a few minutes."

Malkin turned around to warm his back, and Stratos offered him some more of the black brew.

"You think you can hear the Travelling God through…" He would have gestured, but the circumstances prevented it. "All this?"

"Yes."

"You know that whatever it is, it's not a god."

"So they say." Stratos tugged at his monumental beard. Iannis leaned forward and listened intently to the reply coming out of seemingly thin air and manifesting itself in his little wired ear-cup. "But we can hear Him all the same. Every transit, for an hour or so. Sometimes it's very faint, but we're in a good position astronomically right now. The Gates of Heaven are almost overhead in the sky. It's Him."

Malkin blinked. He hadn't heard anything so ridiculous for years, and yet these men – these modern men, with their copper coils and bright spark-gaps, sending and receiving aetheric messages over vast distances with no perceptible delay – clearly believed it.

Iannis turned in his chair. "It's not a secret. Every signaller knows about it, even if they have different opinions as to what it represents. But it repeats in a more or less predictable way."

He put the ear-cup on the desk and fetched a heavy book from a shelf, where it sat with similar volumes. He heaved it open and leafed through the entries in it, all written in an even, rounded letters.

"Here, and forty days later, here." Iannis wetted his thumb and pulled at the parchment. "Forty days. Forty days. It's the same signal, each time. It starts, it repeats, and a couple of days later it stops."

"If it's not a secret, why doesn't everyone know about it?"

"I suppose you have to be a signaller," shrugged Stratos. "This is all quite recent. Only the newest aetheric receivers can hear His voice. It's… a little complicated, but the signal is right at the end of the coil, while we only use the middle, and either side of that, for our messages. You have to go looking for it to find it."

"What does this signal say?" Malkin, despite himself, was intrigued. And it was a distraction from whatever fate he'd receive at the hands of the regional governor.

"The Holy Sequence. The number is the sum of the previous two numbers. One, one, two, three, five, eight, thirteen, twenty-one. Then back to one." Iannis went back to the device, and lifted the pick-up from where it was on the coil to all the way to the left. He listened carefully to his ear-cup, and nodded slowly. He offered it up to Malkin. "Please be respectful of the equipment."

Malkin leaned forward, and Iannis pressed the cup to his ear.

It crackled and hissed, and all Malkin heard was the close rubbing of the folds of his ear against the wooden cup. He took a deep breath and stilled himself – how much easier this would have been if he'd been able to hold it himself against his own head.

There. A faint tone against the wash of the aetheric sea, like stones being dropped into water. Pop pop pop. Pop pop pop pop pop. Pop pop pop pop pop pop pop pop.

He listened to it as it reached twenty-one, heard it go silent for brief interval, then start again. Pop. Pop. Pop pop. Pop pop pop.

Malkin straightened up. "And none of your signallers is, I don't know, carrying out some merry jest on the rest of you?"

"No one has the equipment for that. The signal is strong, and it's the same wherever you go. As if it's coming from the sky, and not the ground." Iannis listened himself for a moment, then set the ear-cup down on the desk. "Are you sure we can't get you something to eat? Whatever's happening out there is taking your bondsman a while to sort out."

"He's not my anything, signaller." There was no rear door to the signalling station, and no windows in the second room either. Malkin stopped being so proud and conceded. "Yes, then. Anything you have. Ylber doesn't care much what condition I arrive in wherever it is I'm going."

"Proussa," reminded Stratos. "I'll see what we have. It won't be much."

He went back through to the front desk, leaving Iannis to disconnect various wires.

"Have you tried talking to Him?" asked Malkin.

"To...?"

"The Travelling God. Or whatever." If they really did think it was the Travelling God, who was Malkin to gainsay that?

"We haven't got the range. Our tiny signals wouldn't reach Him. All this," Iannis spread his arms wide, "and we can barely make ourselves heard twenty miles away. He is, as best we can tell, hundreds of thousands of times further away than that."

Malkin made a face. He couldn't imagine that distance, didn't even know that such a distance could exist. "How far is the sun, then?"

"We think, one hundred and twenty million miles."

Malkin laughed. None of this made any sense. "But you feel the sunlight on your skin, yes? You put your hand out, and it's warmed. If something so far away can still be felt, then why won't your little aether-messages reach up into the sky? What are you afraid of? That He won't answer you?"

Stratos reappeared. He had a bowl with torn slices of flatbreads, a wedge of the sharp cheese that the locals made, and some small fried patties of mashed beans. "It's not much, but you're welcome to it."

"Why won't we talk to the Travelling God, Stratos?" asked Iannis.

"Because we can't." The man set the bowl down on a table. "But we will. Have you heard of the Great Mission, Malkin?"

"Something to do with books of numbers."

"So much more than that. The sum of all knowledge, expressed in a series of calculations. Once it's complete, we'll join the Travelling God at the Gates of Heaven, and we'll enter them together." Stratos read Malkin's expression, and smiled. "You think we're mad, yes? Well, a decade ago, the idea of aetheric messages was just a conjecture. Then it was proved. Then the first equipment was built, and then better equipment, then better still."

"We expect," said Iannis, "that in a few years – call it another ten – a device will exist that'll allow us to talk to the Travelling God. And we don't have to do anything extraordinary to make it happen. It'll just turn up."

"We'll complete the Great Mission," said Stratos, "and achieve Exaltation."

"Ten years? Damn. I'm going to miss it." Malkin couldn't take them seriously. They were fanatics. Well-meaning, and generally benign, but fanatics nevertheless. "Feed me some of that cheese, then."

Stratos did as he was asked, holding the bowl under Malkin's chin to catch the crumbs, alternating with the bread and the bean cakes, which were spicy enough for something to catch in the back of Malkin's throat and cause him to cough into Stratos' beard.

"Sorry about that," he said.

"It'll wash out."

"I'm going to take a look outside," said Iannis, frowning. "It's gone very quiet."

"Be careful," murmured Stratos, as if they were a long-married couple, and perhaps they were.

The older man slipped out of the room, and Malkin took a pause in eating to look around again. Brass and wood and glass had been with them forever, but not configured like this. He swore that he used to understand the world: it had been simple, and if he ran fast enough, his misdeeds always stayed behind him. Now, his crimes were known in places he'd never been, and justice, even the rough kind that Ylber represented, just had to wait for him to show his face.

How was this fair? Why couldn't he have been born a hundred years ago when nonsense like this couldn't happen, when news travelled at the speed of a horse at best, and usually only as far as the end of one jurisdiction and the beginning of another.

The food in Malkin's gut turned sour.

Then Iannis returned. "They've gone. Every one. The bondsmen, whoever else was there."

"Gone where?"

Iannis was apologetic. "That remains to be seen."

The two signallers looked at their guest.

"I'll be on my way, then," said Malkin. "Even with my hands shackled, I suggest you don't try and stop me."

He quickly eased past Iannis in the doorway, through the open counter, and awkwardly worked the latch on the door. It was far brighter outside than in, and it took a few moments for him to see that the signalman had, in fact, been lying. And convincingly enough to fool him.

Ylber tapped his heavy club against his leg. "Now we walk, Malkin. Now we walk."

Malkin looked back at the signalling hut. Iannis was in the doorway, his mouth drawn into a sad smile.

"It seemed wise," he said. "The messengers are fragile, and don't take well to being kicked."

After a moment of considering his options, Malkin snorted. "Well played. Never let it be said that travellers lack cunning."

The signalman made the sign of the Travelling God, which caused some amusement in Ylber's crew in the moments before they set off down the road towards Proussa.

"Laugh all you want, you bastards. They fed me and gave me something to drink. And some of you will still be around when the Travelling God comes. See how you like it then."

Malkin felt a shove in his back, and he stumbled into the first steps of his last journey.

SEVEN
Orbital velocity

How to get used to a non-relativistic universe again, where objects weren't distorted or shifted into invisibility by physics? Everything was crisp and clear and sharp. They had edges. They moved at glacial pace. There was time. Time to calculate, time to manoeuvre, time to just take time. Events rippled symmetrically out from his origin. Causality was restored.

Also, never underestimate the power of continuous thrust. Even with the reduced efficiency necessitated by the loss of one of his radiators, he had slowed from 0.85c in sixty years, to this. It could have, and should have, ended him. For once, everything that could have gone right did. If he ever encountered anything that might have punched a long thin hole through his internal systems, the billion-degree spear of photons that preceded him appeared to have provided protection.

The complex curves of orbital mechanics had unwound, moving his path from a straight line to a heliocentric ellipse, to a graceful planetary circle. PurLeeDah's home world had a new moon, which was him and her.

Simultaneously – it was ironic, given the amount of elapsed time – he had begun broadcasting to the planet below. He'd detected the first tremulous signals fifty years ago. At first, a simple dot sequencing, each group representing a phoneme. The pattern followed recognisable rules that he could map. But without actually hearing a human voice, it remained as abstract as code: these phonemes appeared to mean that concept.

That method of messaging, initially limited to official communications and bureaucratic notes, and only later to letters sent by individual citizens, was slow. It was accurate, however. Repeater stations proliferated across the landmasses. Some were installed on ships: at least, the signals originated from the oceans, although Corbyn couldn't image what kind of boats they were. Not steam powered, judging from the signatures in the atmosphere. The civilisation below seemed... curiously lopsided, as if someone had presented the Khan with a way of keeping in touch with the furthest reaches of his empire, while they themselves continued to live as much as they had done for the previous thousand years, on horseback and in yurts.

There was no evidence of railways, or of buildings taller than a few stories, or of deep mines or long bridges. And there was no sign anything resembling a launchpad. They must have rockets, because the chemical reactions involved in launching something were accidentally easy to create. Look up. Please, look up. After everything, time is short, and I need you to develop space flight before it's too late.

Then the people below began to speak to each other. Conversations, stilted, formal. Still used for point-to-point communications. Here is this information. I have received this information. Corbyn listened, and learned. Language groups appeared as the use of radio spread. What had been mere code were now human voices. Nothing remained of PurLeeDah's tongue, obliterated by ten thousand years of linguistic drift. She would have to learn anew how to speak, if she survived this.

And how was that to happen? How could it possibly happen? To be a civilisation so advanced in one field, and not in another. Something had happened to them to skew them so – did they lack certain minerals? Was there a taboo on technological innovation?

But they had radio. They had the means to power it, and the wit to use it. Corbyn wanted to understand what had happened to them, causing them to turn out in this specific way.

He was going to ask them. More than that. He was going to educate them. Give them the knowledge they needed to race through the next three centuries of development, because while he could be in orbit indefinitely, PurLeeDah would not survive.

How ethical would this be? He was going to just ignore that question. Not only ignore it, he was going to try and tailor their progress to arrive at a singular point: an orbital rendezvous with him, in order to collect PurLeeDah and take her to safety.

Who, though, was he going to ask to help him? All of them? Why not all of them? He would metaphorically clear his throat, and see who might want to talk to him. Someone down there would decide that his mission was a worthy task, and Corbyn would guide them across the generations.

Did they even know he was there?

Where else but the ancient monotheon? The great and the good milled about on its worn flags, occasionally glancing up at the blue dome seemingly suspended in space above them, briefly if grudgingly acknowledging that the devotees of Travelling God may not only have had a point, but they also knew how to build a lasting monument to –

A starship. Called Corbyn.

"Can you even believe this?"

The Lady Berendey looked to her left, and then down, to see the diminutive figure of Mackle, almost nestled within the folds of her court gown. She adjusted her skirt before answering, and brought her shell-rimmed eyeglasses to her nose, just to check who else might be close by: poor eyesight ran in her family like a stain.

"I'm not sure how some of these people gained an invitation," she said. "Especially all the ones proclaiming to be the High Priest of the Travelling God. There must be five, six of them? They can't all be the High Priest, and even if they were, what can they possibly contribute?"

"The issue is," said Mackle, "everyone has claimed some degree of victory, and with it, the moral high ground."

"It's a wonder that there's any room left up there." Lady Berendey scanned the room myopically for both allies and foes. The field of Precursor Studies was small enough that her presence at the gathering was guaranteed, but she also expected to see familiar if unwelcome faces. Mackle was the first she'd seen she might consider a companion. At least, he was harmless enough – his work was tangential to hers – not to be a rival.

"Are you going on the tour of the ancient sites later?" asked Mackle. "I'd like to, but there are a lot of steps."

"The organising committee should be able to find some bright young things to carry you up. And down again, assuming you're not ready for a sky burial."

She smirked, but it was gently meant. Neither of them were in the first flush of youth.

"I'll talk to them." Mackle indicated the end of a row of seats, just one of a great many that had been brought into the monotheon for the occasion. "Shall we sit? My efforts at mingling are already exhausted."

They perched on chairs on adjacent rows. She, struggling to contain the fabric of her skirt that she now regretted wearing. He, with his feet dangling a few inches from the floor.

So many prayers had been made in here. Prayers to a… thing. A vessel that travelled the space between stars as if it were a ship with sails on an ocean, which would not, could not, answer.

Until, of course, now, when she had to deal with all of the repercussions.

"Did you find any corroborating evidence for Corbyn's story?" asked Mackle. He did so quietly, for fear of being overheard.

"We're in the very early stages of translating Precursor script." Lady Berendey kept her voice low and neutral. "Our engines are working all hours to decode the extant inscriptions, but they're so few. Nothing mentioning the Great Honour, or PurLeeDah, or Corbyn's first visit."

"I don't know whether to be disappointed or not."

"After ten thousand years, it's a wonder that there's anything left at all. But given that Corbyn was able – after all our work of the previous decades – to simply tell us what each symbol was, and meant, and how it sounded, it must have gained that knowledge from somewhere." She leaned closer. "I've spent my time, and my money, and my intellect, studying the Precursors. I have a reputation. And now this upstart excuse for a god is trampling all over my hard work. There's a Precursor woman on board, for goodness' sake."

"I thought you'd be excited at the prospect."

She shuddered. "I'm nauseous, is what I am."

Their heads were almost touching. Mackle's broad face wrinkled into a heavy frown. "If we can overcome our philosophical objections to a mechanical mind that is effectively immortal, and our own squeamishness that the natural flora and fauna of our world, including us, is disconnected from our own fossil record and, well, everything. Yes, it's all a bit much, but we have to be brave. When the facts change, we have to change too. Isn't that the way?"

Lady Berendey stared at the floor. She could almost hear the echoes of countless believers around her. Abacuses. The interminable clacking of beads on a frame. Not words, but calculations. She couldn't even complain that they'd been wasting their time. "The travellers have no right to be so smug."

"Of course they don't. Yet what good will it do us to point that out? The trajectory of our whole history has been affected, altered – guided, for the want of a better word – by Corbyn's presence in our night sky for the past however-many thousands of years. Our forebears interpreted the signs as best they could, with the information they had at the time. It's led us to this point, believers and non-believers alike. We are where we are. How we got here is a matter of record."

"Corbyn never once actively interfered with us."

"We did that all on our own. What else could we do?"

"I know. I know." She accepted Mackle's hand patting hers. It was only a small measure of comfort, but welcome all the same. "I feel adrift. Betrayed. The Precursors set this up: if you believe Corbyn, of course. If you can't even trust your ancestors to tell you the truth, then what's the point of them?"

Someone waved enthusiastically to them from across the way. Lady Berendey raised her eyeglasses, and thought she could see Georgieff in the distance. Someone who dressed like Georgieff was most likely to be Georgieff himself.

"Is that...?"

"Yes," confirmed Mackle. He grimaced briefly, before recomposing his face to be more benign.

It was Georgieff, in his trademark garish mismatch of garb that was the opposite of pleasing on the eye. He bowed low, his hat coming off and landing at his feet. "My lady, esteemed colleague."

"Sit down," offered Mackle. "Join the pity party."

"Oh?" Georgieff stooped awkwardly to retrieve his lost item of clothing, and nearly spilled himself onto the floor. "Are we not thrilled at the prospect of our cosmic benefactor bestowing gifts of knowledge on his grateful supplicants?"

"No," said Lady Berendey. "We are not."

Georgieff scraped a chair out of its line and sat opposite the others. "To be honest, neither am I. My government, on the other hand, is quite gung-ho about the idea."

"I've heard similar rumours from some of the other delegates," said Mackle. "Where does the Northern Federation stand?"

Lady Berendey looked momentarily in pain.

"Like that? It's to be expected," said Georgieff. He rolled his hat around in his hands. "This is what happens when our leaders are not scholars. They see the short gains, and not the long costs."

"For them," said Lady Berendey, "there are no long costs. They accelerate into the future, and it's poor souls like us that are left behind. What's the point of study, of exploration, of conjecture, of experimentation, any more? In one fell swoop, we are infantilised."

"No one will stand, because not all will stand," said Mackle. "As long as there is someone willing to take this bargain, everyone will take it, for fear of losing out. Who's going to convince this disparate gathering to refuse Corbyn's offer? Me? You? Who?"

Georgieff nodded. "We are ruined, for certain. And yet, perhaps we can adapt. I mean," and he spread his hands out wide, "we have to adapt. I quite like my life, and I'm ill-suited for anything else than writing and musing and a little light pottering."

"We should approach one of the High Priests and ask to take the blue, then." Lady Berendey felt her dander rise. "If we're going to admit defeat, we may as well throw our lot in with the enemy wholeheartedly."

"It won't come to that. There's much of a practical nature we can do." Georgieff was conciliatory. "Our students accept they know less than we do, and yet seem content to learn from us. Some enforced humility is difficult, but we can all remember what it was like to be taught by a wiser practitioner, can't we?"

"It's not humility. It's humiliating, sir, that's what it is. Some of us have made whole careers out of, apparently, being wrong about everything, or at the very least, being too stupid not to have found so many obvious answers. You, me, everybody here. Gainsaid by a..." She sputtered to a halt.

"By a machine."

"By a machine."

"It's difficult for all of us," said Mackle. "But what can we do? Corbyn is an immensely old mind, carrying with it the knowledge of untold complexity from beyond the stars, as well as considerable information on this world and its past. Moreover, it has, or claims to have, one of our ancestors, still alive after all this time. And while, granted, it admits to not knowing everything, for the purposes of this juncture in our development, it may as well be a literal god."

"And we're just going to bow down to it? Worship it? Is that what you recommend?" She jerked to her feet. "Never. Some of us will keep our dignity, and our principles."

She deliberately pushed through the gap between Georgieff and Mackle, and stamped off into the far recesses of the monotheon, where she seethed in silence, and as far as she could tell, in private. There were hundreds of learned people gathered here, and what was the point? Mackle was right: it had already been decided. Those who would listen to Corbyn's lectures would learn the secrets of the ancients. Those who wouldn't were doomed to be stuck in the present.

No people, however they were governed, by despot or democracy, would stand for the latter.

"My lady?"

She turned on her heel to confront this impertinent fool who'd interrupted her fugue.

A woman, shorter, younger, and darker than she, dressed in dark wool from neck to ankle, made a small acknowledgement with a dip and tilt of her head.

"What? What is it? And who are you?"

"I'm with the organising committee. My usual job is helping with the upkeep of the historic buildings in the city – a conservator, if you wish – but I've been co-opted into helping at this meeting."

"A guide? What would I want with a guide right now?"

"I'm more than willing to act as your guide, my lady. But I come with a different offer."

"For goodness' sake, out with it. I haven't got the time, or the patience, for games."

The woman seemed to steel herself. "Corbyn would like to speak to you."

Lady Berendey's anger, her refractory recalcitrance, blunted the woman's words enough that it took a few more moments for the import of them to pierce through.

"To me?"

"Yes. To you."

"And it asked for me by name?"

"Yes. He did."

"How does it know who I am?" There were millions of souls in the world, tens of thousands in this mountain city alone, and hundreds at the gathering under the blue dome.

"You can ask him."

"Him?"

"That's how he refers to himself. In our language, at least. It might be different in others." The woman took a step back. "If you're willing, you can follow me now."

Lady Berendey's composure was tattered, but not completely torn. She gathered up what was left of it along with her skirts, and indicated that, yes, she was reluctantly willing, and assuredly against her better judgement. The reason for all her discomfort and anxiety wanted to talk to her.

She went through every emotion as she walked behind the woman who was now exactly her guide, around a part-circumference of the monotheon, and through a door into a corridor, and up some stairs to another room: a big room, possibly a repurposed refectory or some such, complete with long tables and benches, dark with age.

Aetheric messaging equipment was set up at several discrete stations, each one with its own soundproofed booth constructed from quilted screens. The air smelled of that bright, fresh, slightly sharp odour emitted by voltaic piles, and it made the inside of her nose twitch.

Her guide led her to one of the stations. A signalman – barely a man, a boy whose face wore a desperate and insubstantial beard – got up as they approached, and gave up his space at the bench.

"Are we ready?"

"Yes, yes." The signalman saw the volume of Lady Berendey's skirt and heaved the bench out further from the table. "He's waiting."

Still nonplussed, Lady Berendey eased herself into position.

"You put this to your ear," said the signalman, holding up the ear-cup, "and speak into –"

"I know how a messenger works, thank you. That will be all."

"If you have any problems, then –"

"I'll be sure to let you know. Now, if you don't mind?"

Her nerves were getting the better of her, making her sharper and more brittle. But that didn't mean she was any less angry with the Travelling God. She faced the equipment, the long coil with its contacts, and tried to blot out everything else around her. The screens did help: they muffled the low conversations that were happening around her, and gave her a welcome sense of isolation, if not intimacy. She took up the ear-cup and held it to her ear, and leaned forward towards the speaking device, hoisted onto a stand so that it was already level with her mouth.

She listened for a moment. What did she expect to hear? Breathing? She was talking to a machine. An it. She'd be better off searching for signs of life in a calculating engine.

"Hello?"

"Lady Magda Berendey. Thank you for agreeing to talk to me."

It was it. Him. Corbyn. The Travelling God. It was difficult not to feel a little overwhelmed. There was a light in the sky that her ancestors had worshipped, and now she was sitting down and having a conversation with it.

"I... how private is this? Can anyone with a receiver not just listen in and hear what we have to say to each other?"

"Theoretically yes. But I have narrowcast this transmission, and we are using a frequency not usually utilised. We can hop to another frequency, repeatedly, which will make eavesdropping impractical. The operators already have this in hand if required."

His – its – voice was indistinguishable from human. Its language was flawless and idiomatic. Its vocabulary was dense and technical.

"What do you look like?" she asked.

"A chimney. A very tall chimney. I am hollow from top to bottom. All my structures and services are built into the walls. I am designed to gather fuel from what you know as the aether, compress it until it burns, and expel the hot gas out behind me, pushing myself forwards, as much as a rocket does. In addition, I have broad sails like a windmill, not used to generate power, but to shed the excess of it. I also have the crew module of the spaceship The Great Honour, which I salvaged, along with PurLeeDah, who I know you are aware of. It is small in comparison to my size, but it protrudes from my hull. Does this answer your question fully?"

"But that's not you, is it?"

"It is as much me, as your body is you. Your brain is a double-handful of wet jelly inside your skull, yet you would not call it you, any more than you would call your heart you, or your stomach you. My mind is a crystalline matrix into which has been imprinted both personality and functionality, but if I jettisoned my vessel and all my sensory inputs, I would be a fundamentally different being. These are deep philosophical questions, but I am convinced by experience and argument that the substance which is I is indivisible from the substance which is me."

Lady Berendey took several steadying breaths. "Do you know how much damage you've caused?"

"PurLeeDah wished to be returned to her home world, despite the passage of time. I offered an alternative, namely to find an already-technologically advanced civilisation, in the hope that they would be able to help me shed my excess velocity swiftly and safely. She insisted, and I complied without considering the effects my persistent presence in your sky would have on your nascent culture. This was my mistake, and I apologise for that. You may have developed very differently otherwise."

"We worshipped you as a god!"

"That is true. On my own home world, where humans first evolved, gods were a universal phenomenon that occurred across their entire geographical range, across their entire history. You would certainly have had your gods without my intervention. Broadly speaking, that you had just one god throughout may be unique. Again, for the record, I am not a god, although I understand why it might have looked that way."

She needed to focus. She couldn't afford to be awed by the fact that she was talking to the Travelling God, talking to him as if he was simply in the next town, and they had booked a five minute slot to exchange family news.

"You're proposing to give us scientific knowledge, yes?"

"Yes. And in return, when you are ready, you will fly up into orbit and rescue PurLeeDah. I estimate that this will take, from where you are currently, some two centuries." Corbyn seemed confident in his timescale, even though she'd be long gone by then. "I had hoped that you would be ready by the time I had slowed sufficiently to orbit your world, that we would meet each other there in the aether. I had to expedite my braking manoeuvres. After ten thousand years, the machines that keep PurLeeDah alive but asleep are failing. She is dying, Lady Berendey. The one I have promised to protect and deliver safely to her people is dying, and this is the only thing I can do to keep my word. Do you understand?"

"I do understand, but do you understand that by doing this you'll destroy us completely?"

"Explain your thinking."

"We... Look, Corbyn – I can call you Corbyn, can't I?"

"That is my given name."

"Corbyn. Whatever we've done up until now has been our own creation. Yes, we told stories about the Travelling God, but they were our stories. We owned them. They were ours, not yours. You couldn't communicate with us, so we just had to guess at what you represented, what you wanted, how we were to live. We eventually dethroned you. You stopped being an object of devotion for most of us, and became a scientific curiosity." She gathered up her courage. "But it was our science. Using our minds. At our pace. Everything that we know, we've had to wrestle from the sky, or from the ground, or from our own bodies. And you, in one fell swoop, would bring all that crashing down."

"You were once able to build a starship that was more advanced that I am. You have lost so much."

"Then let us find it again for ourselves!" She realised that she was shouting, and composed herself. "Do you know of the Great Mission, Corbyn?"

"I have been made aware of it."

"That was us. Working our way to the stars. If you tell us everything we need to know to do that, it's a perversion of that ideal. It won't be our achievement. We won't have pride in it. It'll just be you, using us. For goodness' sake, Corbyn: ten thousand years have passed since we could do the great things you say we could. We're a completely different people now, and we're not ready for this. We're not ready at all. You say that you're not a god."

"I am not a god."

"Then don't act like one. I'm sorry for PurLeeDah. I'm sorry for you. I'm sorry she'll die after all this time and leave you alone. But we can't bear this weight. It'll crush us. It'll be all our ends. If you're not a god, then don't be a god. Please."

There was a moment of dead air, nothing but a static hiss like waves on a distant shore.

"Thank you for your words, Lady Berendey. I will consider them most carefully."

She heard a click. She put the ear-cup down, and leaned back from the desk. She looked around, momentarily surprised at her mundane surroundings, the padded screens, the aetheric devices, the vaulted ceiling, the much-scrubbed and graffitied tabletops.

Slowly, the enormity of what she'd done, what she'd said, became clear to her, and she wavered, swaying enough that her guide, who may or may have been there throughout, gently took her elbow and steadied her.

"I'm fine," she said. "I'm fine. If you could escort me back to the monotheon, I'd be grateful. I believe the first session will be starting soon."

Eight
Stationary

Corbyn watched the robot drag PurLeeDah from the sleep tank because she was too weak to manage it herself. This is the end, he thought. This cannot continue. The robot used its manipulators to slap her on the back, to encourage her to cough out the remains of the gel, and again when she was finally breathing, to gently wipe her face so that she could see.

"What's happening? Corbyn? Why am I like this?"

"You are some fifteen hundred years older than when you were last awake. This technology has preserved your biological functions astonishingly well, I am certain far exceeding the expectations of those who made it – but it has begun to fail. So now you are awake, and you will not be returning to the tank. You must eat and drink and exercise. You have to gain weight and muscle mass, or else you will perish."

She sat on the deck, head down, propped up against the robot's crouching body, watching the gel drip from her body and through the perforated floor.

"Have they come for me?"

"No. And they will not be coming for you. Either we are too early, or they are too late. Their civilisation is extraordinary, for reasons that I will come to, but they are not sufficiently advanced to achieve space flight in any capacity, and will not do so for several centuries. PurLeeDah, there is much to explain, but we have to see to your care first."

The robot carried her to the next room, the one with the bolted down table and bench seat, and parked her there while it spidered off to collect a set of coveralls, consisting of a fabric that was now thousands of years old. It fell into dust as the robot tried to move them. Not quite believing that its task was no longer possible, the robot mimed as if it was still holding the clothes, before staring blankly at the cascade of particles settling on the floor.

Corbyn, through the robot's cameras, recognised that this was not a good sign.

The water was still potable. It had a very simple chemical formula, and if all else had failed he could have synthesised it from his own hydrogen reserves, and the oxygen that had come with the Great Honour's crew section. The robot handed her a mug of it, and Corbyn tweaked the cabin temperature up to compensate for the fact that PurLeeDah was going to be naked for a while.

The food – Corbyn had no way of knowing if it was palatable. Bland and nutritious would have sufficed, but what if it was now toxic? Amino acids, minerals, vitamins: some would survive indefinitely, but some would break down, and the daughter chemicals would have contaminated whatever they were in. She was willing to try. He was less willing to let her.

It was just water for now. She ran her hand through her thinning hair, and inspected the still-sticky strands caught between her fingers.

"Where are we now, Corbyn?"

"I have shed my excess velocity. I am currently in orbit around your home planet. There is a thriving, vibrant multipolity civilisation below, largely peaceful and curious. They developed radio some years ago, and I am now in communication with some of them. You would be fascinated by them, and in turn, they would be fascinated by you. There are, however, complications."

"How large are the complications?"

"Insurmountable, at first consideration. I have offered them the knowledge they require to quickly gain orbital lift capability – quickly in this context is somewhere between one and two centuries of accelerated progress. The most persuasive voices amongst their intellectual class have convinced me that it would be grossly unethical to proceed with this plan. I have already had an unwittingly enormous impact on their society, and to insert myself so completely into their scientific, economic, and social development would likely cause the simultaneous collapse of all three. You are the historian: I would value your opinion."

"I'm tired, Corbyn. All I wanted to do was go home."

"I am also tired, PurLeeDah. I am damaged, and my own systems are beginning to show their age."

"A machine shouldn't get tired," she said.

"I have become something more than a machine. I don't know what. I will leave that for others to judge. Your postcedents worshipped me as a god, although that time has now passed. Largely. There are still cultists, some of them influential, especially now that I have made contact."

"A god? That… doesn't make any sense."

"I can explain, although the explanation will require further explanations." Corbyn hesitated, and because he so rarely hesitated, PurLeeDah, even in her reduced state, looked up and into the robot's cameras.

"What's wrong?"

"Do you trust me?"

"As far as someone is ever able to trust another being, yes. Unequivocally. That doesn't answer my question, though. Corbyn?"

"You will have to trust me on this. Before you die, you will breathe good air again, and eat good food, and drink good drink, and you will do it in good company, and for a long time. The calculations are complex, but fortunately, that is what I was built for. I am confident that I can do this for you, PurLeeDah. You are going home."

She kept on asking him how, and he kept on asking her if she trusted him. He was clearly doing... something. Noises hitherto unheard rattled around the module, sometimes persistently for hours at an end, and sometimes just once, and so sudden, that she couldn't help but jump.

She was weak. Lethargic. Once upon a time, she would have put up a better argument, demanding to know what was going on outside, and not putting up with such mealy-mouthed responses. Of course she trusted him. He had saved her from two fates worse than death – being entombed in a disintegrating spaceship travelling through the wilds of uncharted space, and being deliberated killed by the shadow crew installed without her knowledge by a government so intent on controlling the narrative of her journey that they were willing to commit murder. He had sided with her at every turn, and at considerable personal cost.

He might not be a god, but he was definitely a person.

So, no. She didn't know what he was building, for surely he was building, and she didn't know to what purpose, and she was too tired to press him on it.

Objectively, she knew the signs of malnutrition, both internally and externally. Her limbs were thin, not skeletal thin, but lacking the muscle and fat that her own body was digesting in order to keep the rest of her alive. She felt hollow, and yet not actually hungry. It would take effort to eat, and honestly, it seemed like too much effort, even if there was something for her to put in her mouth, even if it might kill her.

She slept fitfully. The floor was hard on her bones. The booming and clattering from Corbyn's project kept waking her up, and she complained, and he soothed her, but he never once stopped for her ease.

Again, objectively, she realised that there was sudden and needful haste, but what she wanted now was just to fall into a soft bed and dream forever. The sleep tank looked so incredibly inviting, but it would be no more than a coffin now. It would kill her. As would not going back in the sleep tank.

She made no decisions, either to do or not do. The robot kept pressing water on her, encouraging her to do simple but exhausting stretches, to engage in hand games and puzzles. She did them because it was Corbyn, not because she wanted to or had any interest in the outcomes.

He talked to her about what he had gleaned from his conversations with the people on the surface. Yes, they had worshipped him, or rather his sign in their sky, as a god. They called him the Travelling God, and they had constructed a whole religion around the Cherenkov radiation he emitted as he barrelled into the solar wind at something just less than light speed. They had taken the colour blue to be sacred. They had become highly proficient in mathematics far earlier than they would otherwise have done. They expressed their devotion by means of increasingly complex calculations. They formulated the Great Mission: by describing the universe in terms of tabulated numbers, they would achieve something called Exaltation.

Some still believed that. Corbyn didn't say whether or not he was disabusing them of that notion. She half-heartedly chided him, telling him that it wasn't good that he was leading them on. He replied gnomically, saying only that the Travelling God cultists were key to his whole plan.

When she asked him again what the plan was, he again asked her to trust him. The noises off, the vibrations that rattled the panels in her module, continued unabated.

She wasn't sure how many hours or days – it couldn't have been weeks or months because that would have killed her – passed before the banging finally ceased. She noticed its absence more than she had noted its presence.

"Corbyn?"

"PurLeeDah. Everything is ready. I am ready, and you need to be too."

The robot skittered around the module, accessing behind panels, redogging them, checking statuses, and closing down the sleep tanks. Their lights had been a constant throughout, the green and the amber and the red. Now they were just off. Somewhere below her feet, a pump chugged and a servo popped.

"Can you tell me now?"

"I can, because you have to play your part in this. I did not know whether this was going to work – rather, I knew my part of it would theoretically work, but a practical experiment was required before I was willing to risk your life on it – and there are also some human factors involved. I cannot ever remember willingly committing a crime before, simply because the situation has never arisen in which I came across anything resembling a jurisdiction. However, given the strength of sentiment against my further interference with your home world, I decided that some degree of caution was necessary. But the followers of the Travelling God are used to acting below the level of usual governmental notice, and it will take the authorities considerable time, if they ever do, to catch up with you. You will be among fierce protectors, PurLeeDah, and hopefully, eventually, among friends."

"This explains nothing, Corbyn," she complained.

"The preamble was necessary. Now, to be plain." The robot stopped its wanderings, and folded itself into the corner of the room. It recentred its lenses on her, but even then, seemed to somehow radiate a nervous tension, of something monumental about to happen and not yet realised.

"Given that I am a deep-space vessel a kilometre long, I was never meant to enter an atmosphere, let alone touch down on a planet's surface. The primary reason for this is that my drive is based around the collection of interstellar hydrogen which I then use to fuel a hydrogen-hydrogen fusion reaction, which in turn provides my thrust. While I do not emit long lived radionuclides in my exhaust, the amount of prompt radiation is considerable. Given this, I had discounted any scenario which might involve dropping below the Karman line.

"However. There is something called the Kittinger manoeuvre. Its various dynamics have been widely explored, usually out of necessity. It is a way of delivering a human payload to a planetary body by means of free fall descent, arresting the descent velocity by means of parachute or other device. In order for this to be practicable, the orbital component of the delivery system must become stationary with respect to the target site below."

PurLeeDah interrupted. "This is not plain, Corbyn. This is not plain. I'm sure you've been very clever, so just tell me."

"In essence, I will make a retrograde burn just above the atmosphere. I will achieve a dead stop, and fall below the Karman line into your planet's mesosphere. Once there, I will extend a boom on which your module is now attached, and then release you. Once free of the boom, a balloon filled with hydrogen gas will provide this module with buoyancy, expediting your controlled descent. I have checked my numbers repeatedly, and am confident that I have allowed sufficient margins for contingencies.

"The remaining issue is me. I will also be in free fall. Left in such a state, I will nominally strike the surface in two and half minutes – it will be longer, given the drag effect of the thickening atmosphere, but nevertheless soon after. In order to activate the D-jump mechanism safely, I have to ensure a minimum distance from you within that time-frame. I believe I can achieve that before my impact."

She stirred, and sat up fully. "And if you don't?"

"The Kittinger manoeuvre has always prioritised the human crew over the orbital component. Admittedly, as far as my records are concerned, it has never been attempted by a sentient spaceship before. But I am prepared for things to go wrong."

"You'll die."

"And you will live."

"There has to be another way."

"Unfortunately, given the timescales in which we must work, no. And given that I was always willing to sacrifice myself for you, and that you would strenuously object to that, I have already begun my final approach. You will hear my drive make a short burn, and gravity will become complicated. One last instruction: the Travelling God cultists who will track your descent and recover you from the module are aware that you do not share a mutually comprehensible language. Please be compliant to their gestural instructions. You have been without human company for so very long, and it will feel strange."

The deck began to vibrate, and down began to shift. The robot spread its legs wide and made its way to her, and over her, and held her tight in its embrace. She clung to it.

She felt everything move, and then nothing. She was weightless.

"The umbilical connections to Corbyn have been severed," said the intercom, with Corbyn's voice. "We are a separate entity now. Please remain calm."

She was falling through the sky, rather than falling through space.

There was a noise like the wind, a soft, tearing sound, intermittent and then continuous.

"Pumping hydrogen," said the intercom. "You will feel deceleration."

And just like that, her empty guts began to settle, and the vertiginous whirl in her head subsided. Even the most subtle of clues as to down and up was sufficient.

"Corbyn? Is Corbyn safe?"

"I am no longer in contact with Corbyn."

What did that mean? Surely, there hadn't been enough time for him to have either escaped gravity, or not. He should still be there, close by. But there were no windows, no reason for there to be windows. She couldn't see out. She'd not seen out for thousands of years, and it was only now she suddenly felt the lack.

The sound of air rushing past them grew louder. Then the module began to swing like a pendulum.

"Is that normal?"

"Vortex shedding has caused us to oscillate. It should not be dangerous. Please remain calm."

There was nothing she could do now. There had been nothing she could do then, either, but at least Corbyn had listened to her, took her opinions into account. He had seemed in charge of the physical world outside, no matter how illusory his control had been in reality.

But this was nature. She was falling from the edge of space to the ground, attached to a bag of hydrogen above her. There was weather. She hadn't experienced weather for so long.

"How do I get out of here?" she asked.

"That has been planned. Touchdown estimated in nine minutes. Hydrogen is reaching full capacity. Our velocity will decrease shortly. Please remain calm."

All of this had happened so quickly, she hadn't had time to be anxious. Which was probably intended. But now she could feel it. The tightness in her chest, the roar in her ears, the tingling in her limbs. Just short of panic. The only real things were the robot's confining embrace and her grip on its leg.

The module continued to swing back and forth alarmingly. She began to feel nauseous on top of everything, even though she only had water to bring back up. There was a flood of acid in her stomach that presaged vomiting.

"Make it stop. Make it stop."

"The amplitude of the oscillations is within expected tolerances. They will decrease as we encounter thicker air. Please remain calm."

She didn't know if she could. She was buzzing, almost vibrating with fear. After everything she'd been through. After everything, to end it like this. She didn't even know what she would be dashed against, except that it would be fast and final.

But the robot, the intercom, the whatever, was right. The wind noise began to quieten. The wild swinging became less extreme. The knot in her guts slowly unwound.

"This bot must move. Remain sitting. Remain calm."

The robot extricated itself gradually, and the last leg to move was the one she was clinging to. She was tempted to hold on, meaning that she would be dragged naked across the mesh floor. She reluctantly let its smooth carapace slip from her grasp, and watched it as it picked its way across the module to the door. The door had once led into an airlock. She didn't know what lay beyond now.

The rocking motion of the floor caused the bot to skitter. Sea legs. It hadn't got its sea legs, and neither had she. It braced itself across the width of the door.

"Avert your eyes. The light will be very bright and may cause photokeratitis. Please remain calm."

She did so, turning to face the far wall. Her shadow, and that of the bot, was abruptly and momentarily imprinted on it. A pop. A great swelling of air. A rush of sound. A garden of perfumes. A wash of warm yellow light.

"You may now approach, but carefully."

She was almost too scared to turn back around. She was still sitting, and she shuffled around.

The bot was guarding the place where the door had once been. There was nothing else but a soft blue. And clouds. There were clouds. She remembered them.

She crawled over, ignoring how hard the floor was on her knees. The vista grew larger. A horizon. A deeper blue, almost grey, flecked with white. The sea. The ocean.

"Oh." She breathed deeply. The complex scents and tastes of home. She was home.

She came closer, reaching out for the bot's legs again, holding on to them and using them to haul herself half upright. There was a whole world outside, and she was now drifting with the wind.

"Four minutes until touch down."

She was cold, and she didn't care. There was a step where there had once been a door, and that step was so very high.

"Corbyn?"

"By now, Corbyn will have either D-jumped away, or impacted the ocean. I have no information on his status."

"Why not? How can he leave me guessing like this?"

"Neither do I have information on his motivations. But please remain calm."

"I am calm! I'm also angry and disappointed and sad and scared. I can be all of those things." She squeezed the bot's legs with her hands, and if it felt anything, it showed no reaction, and the intercom remained silent. "This is the sea. Where's the land?"

"Corbyn determined a descent over water would minimise local damage if anything went wrong. A ship, crewed by Travelling God cultists, is coming for you. My cameras ascertain that they are currently some six kilometres upwind of the landing site. If you look down, you will be able to see them for yourself."

PurLeeDah edged forward fractionally, towards the vertiginous drop, and yes, below her was a ship. She had no idea what she had imagined that ship to look like, but this one? This one was a sailing ship. A fat-hulled two-masted wooden sailing ship, the like of which she'd never seen before and had only heard about in stories so old they hadn't even been written on her planet, but another planet that was light years away and centuries in the past.

Now those centuries were millennia, and there were cogs and caravels on her seas.

Its white sails were furled, and the ship, like her, was drifting. She couldn't see the crew, but as she watched a great sheet dropped from the crossbeam of the highest mast and puffed out. A wake began to glitter white behind it.

"They have spotted you, and will be on station shortly."

"Do I wait in here?" She asked. That seemed unlikely. There was now no door, and nothing to prevent the water from rushing in. "Do I have to swim?"

She didn't have the strength to swim, even if she could remember how. Corbyn must have planned for this. Corbyn planned for everything, and left nothing to chance.

"What do I do?"

"There is a raft attached to the side of the module. It is semi-rigid inflatable boat, which you must enter, on or shortly after touchdown. This module will be held up by the hydrogen balloon for a brief period, but it must be jettisoned quickly, as it will drag the module unpredictably and make egress difficult. It will also then begin to sink." The intercom paused. "One minute until touchdown. Please move away from the doorway and remain calm."

She pushed herself backwards, and the bot clambered outside and out of sight. The quality of sound changed. No longer dominated by the wind, there was a component of waves in it, an overwhelming and mighty rumble.

"Thirty seconds," said the intercom. "Brace."

There was nothing but the bolted-down table and bench to brace herself with, so that was what she did, sliding onto the seat and holding on edges, pressing herself down and ready for a jarring collision with the iron-hard ocean.

When it came, it was barely a kiss. Suddenly, the sea was at her doorstep, and a moment later, the bot reappeared. It held the small white boat against the water's surface with two of its limbs, the door frame with another two, and with two more, it beckoned to her.

"Quickly," said the intercom.

She stood up, and was scooped away out of her seat, firmly and at speed, but never deliberately painfully, even though it did hurt her thin skin and hard bones. She slithered into the bottom of the boat, already wet with spray, already chill despite the hard sun overhead. She rolled onto her back, and gawped at the vast balloon suspended above her.

It was untethered. It floated away, free, fast, but already deflating. The module lurched, and she looked back at it, industrial pipework on its surface, abruptly terminating where it had been severed. Pale. Brittle. Yellowing.

The bot pushed her away. The boat rocked, and she fell flat again.

She hurried to her elbows, and the module was already half drowned. The bot, pinioned in the doorway, turned its cameras from her, up towards the sky, then back to her for one last look. It disappeared beneath the swell. Bubbles.

Then it was gone and she was alone on the ocean.

The unfamiliar motion of the waves made it impossible to stand, and almost as difficult to sit up, but she eventually scrambled her hands against the smooth plastic topside sufficiently to kneel up. There followed moments when she was convinced that she had been abandoned, that she had been missed and would never be found again.

But then she saw the sail, and despite everything that had happened to her before, or would happen after, she managed to raise her hand to it, and hold it there, until she was finally saved.

ᚾᛁᚾᛖ Nine
Velocity to be determined

Corbyn was done. It was over, a lifetime's work – lifetimes of work – and now what was he supposed to do? Of all the emotions he had unexpectedly experienced, this was the most... what word would he use here? Intense? If he had a heart, there would be hole there now.

He should feel some measure of satisfaction, of a job not just well done, but finessed and finagled out of seemingly nowhere. He should not have succeeded. He should have failed, over and over again. So many modes of failure, so many moments where he ought to have been filtered out of existence.

He didn't know why he had slipped through the exceedingly fine mesh. Blind chance, or something more? Providence? He had carefully curated his efforts, and had calculated his way to shifting the odds in his favour. Had he made his own luck? For certain, if he had made different decisions, then he would never have reached this end point. Was that it, then? Had he inadvertently hit the right combination to an astronomical puzzle of incredible complexity, and had done so in real time?

If there had been a million Corbyns and a million PurLeeDahs attempting the same manoeuvre a million different ways, his was the only one that could possibly have worked. So why was he not more pleased? He was a machine mind designed to solve problems. He had hit the jackpot.

Why did it hurt so much?

He drifted. Having matched all the vectors for that one moment of stillness, of falling, of sensing something outside of his hull that wasn't for once the vacuum of space, he had delivered his cargo, then counted out the seconds of separation before he D-jumped away in a thunderclap that would have echoed across the ocean. Then he was here, in the lee of the planet's orbit, moving at the same velocity as it, little more than cosmic flotsam.

Had she heard him? He didn't know. He had purposefully left all the last few details to his bot. It was dumb, but it could follow instructions. The temptation to keep watching her even as he ploughed at terminal speed into the waves would have been too great. He knew his weaknesses. He was self-aware and actualised. If he didn't know what it was to care, then he knew enough about it to imitate the emotion so completely that it was indistinguishable from the real thing. Even he was unable to tell them apart.

But she had been put in the boat, and her rescue was imminent. His bot had told him that, moments before it went offline. Drowned. While it was trivial to protect a device from a vacuum, it was profoundly difficult to do so against immersion. Every ten metres meant another bar of pressure, and water and electricity were inimical. He had sacrificed the bot. He had sacrificed much of his repair material. It had been enough. It had been sufficient. He had not had to sacrifice himself.

He had done everything right, and it still hurt.

He missed her. He would go on missing her. There would be years ahead in which to miss her. Decades. Centuries, if he lasted that long.

Earth had given him a mission. He had failed at that. Spectacularly. PurLeeDah had given him another. He had run with that as if his life depended on it, even though it hadn't. It had, though, been something to latch on to, giving him purpose, offering him the opportunity to prove that he could do something. It had offered him redemption. He had sought her forgiveness. He had been granted it. He had made amends, in some small part, for the errors of the past.

And it was over. It was over, and now what was he to do?

She would grow old and die. So would he. Just on different time scales, as if he was always moving quicker, shifting his inertial frame to ever higher values of gamma, while she was where she wanted to be, rooted to the world where she was born, moving into the future a mere one second at a time.

Well, then. If she had thought that returning to where she had come from was so important, across time and space and everything in between, then perhaps it should be important to him too. Notions of home stirred. Wherever it was.

He opened his cameras to the stars, and started to plot his course.

About the Author

Simon Morden trained as a planetary geologist, realised he was never going to get into space, and decided to write about it instead. His writing career includes a mix of short stories, novellas and novels which blend science fiction, fantasy and horror, a five-year stint as an editor for the British Science Fiction Association, a judge for the Arthur C Clarke Awards, and regular speaking engagements at the Greenbelt arts festival.

His novel *Another War* (2005) was shortlisted for a World Fantasy Award, and the first three books starring sweary Russian scientist Samuil Petrovitch (*Equations of Life*, *Theories of Flight*, and *Degrees of Freedom*) were published in three months of each other in 2011; collectively they won the Philip K Dick Award.

Simon is having an eclectic late career: recent non-fiction includes *The Red Planet*, a mostly complete and almost entirely factual natural history of Mars, a Radio 4 thinkpiece, and an academic paper for the Institutions of Extraterrestrial Liberty, while fiction currently involves the hard *SF Gallowglass* and *The Flight of the Aphrodite* (both from Gollancz), and the Belhaven fantasy series published via his own Fell Books imprint. He's lived in Gateshead for over 30 years, but is now permanently resigned to 'not coming from round here'.

ALSO FROM NEWCON PRESS

ANIMALS – Geoff Ryman
A powerful new novel from the multiple award-winning author of *HIM*, *Was* and *The Child Garden* The chilling tale of a family caught at the heart of a terrifying and transformative epidemic; an astonishing fusion of beautiful writing and pure horror as the world we know falls apart.

The Hamlet – Joanna Corrance
A fabulous tale that dances between horror and science fiction with an added dash of weird, *The Hamlet* is a mosaic featuring the inter-linked lives of inhabitants of a very peculiar rural community during the time when 'things got strange', and shows us the consequences of that strangeness.

Rowany de Vere and a Fair Degree of Frost – Chaz Brenchley Rowany has taken up service on Mars. As a spy. Her mission is to escort a defector across the hostile surface of Mars, pursued by Russian agents. Success will require every ounce of her skills, but she is Rowany de Vere. Of the Colonial Office.

The Other Frankenstein – Melissa F. Olson
Elizabeth Frankenstein and Heck Saville's parallel, intersecting stories encompass murder, loss, trauma and ultimately empowerment, in this stunning tale, an enthralling feminist saga that uses the classic tale of *Frankenstein* as a springboard and weaves a potent tale of horror, love, and revenge.

www.newconpress.co.uk